NORTHERN BEACHES WRITERS' GROUP

The Northern Beaches Writers' Group is an award-winning writing critique group based in Sydney. We're online at:

northernbeacheswritersgroup.com
facebook.com/northernbeacheswritersgroup

edited by

ZENA SHAPTER

Rhapsody

First published in Australia 2021 by
the Northern Beaches Writers' Group, Sydney.

Cover design & internal design by Zena Shapter.

The characters in this book are fictitious and any resemblance to real
persons, living or dead, is purely coincidental.

Contents

Do You Hear the People Sing? – Sonia Zadro – 9

Case 65726: The Lighthopper – Azmeena Kelly – 20

The Search – Tara Ray – 31

Song For A Moment In Time – Susan Steggall – 44

The Air You Get – Zena Shapter – 59

Hotel Coolangatta – Kate Mitchell – 70

Honey Coming Back – Peter Fagan – 81

True Believers – Phil Burgin – 96

King, King Calowe – Millicent Davis – 107

The Need For Witchcraft – Guy Hallowes – 120

Treachery – Elise Robertson – 126

I Don't Believe in Yesterday – Howard Reid – 143

Brothers in Arms – Rose Saltman – 153

2001, A Space Operetta – Mijmark – 164

Message in a Bottle – Rodney Jensen – 198

Acknowledgements – 203

Also by the Northern Beaches Writers' Group – 205

Because lyrics are magical

Do You Hear the People Sing?

Sonia Zadro

The monster beat me, again and again, making me scream and cry out until I shot up in the darkness, wide awake, banging my head hard on the park bench seat. I shoved my sleeping bag away and wiped away the sweat from my beard and hair, longer and more matted than ever.

"Damn!" I rubbed the bruise on my head, trying to ease the pain. "Damn, Fucking Fuck!"

My bottle of whiskey nearly empty, I swallowed the last mouthful and tucked back into my old sleeping bag. Centennial Park was freezing tonight. Fog sat quietly around the bare branches and hovered over the lake, where ducks huddled together in their sleep. The landscape was calm and beautiful, belying the tumult inside my head. Even the sky was clear and pure with its full moon setting all afire with preternatural light.

It had been twelve years since I left Margaret, and that bastard of an uncle still plagued my nights. I'd never told Margaret about him. I'd never told a soul. Some things are not meant to be told – they live in a place so far down, so tight and burrowed away, that sometimes you don't even know if they're real anymore.

But keeping the secret about Uncle Mic had done me no favours. It seemed the longer I shoved it away, the more power that bastard held over me. If I allowed myself to be honest, the monster I became around Margaret was halfway as bad as the bastard who had tied me up in the back study every Friday night till I was fourteen, making me do things, unspeakable things, and leaving me sick with fear and shame for the things he made me do.

I shook my head. How stupid do your parents have to be? How could Uncle Mic be helping me with my homework when, year after year after year, I kept failing at school?

But I never told. I never dared tell anyone. I couldn't risk waking up to dead parents, strangled to death, or with their throats cut.

That's what he said would happen.

"Want pills, Golly?"

I startled and hit my head again on the bench seat. "For God's sake! Why do you always do that Fran? You know I've got the jitters!"

"They'll get you some sleep at least?"

The strong wiry old woman had been a friend for several years now and, despite believing herself to be a witch, her strength and constant presence had saved me. I looked at the pills she held out and shoved them away. "One addiction is enough."

"When are you going to sort out those demons? I'd like some

sleep too you know, I can hear you all the way to the lake. You half frightened those ducks to death, you did."

"When I'm dead, Franny, good and dead." I lay back down and nestled again into my bag.

I had tried to kill myself, once with pills, another time I tried to drown myself over at Coogee on a wild summer's night. Every night since, I'd tried with drink. I was rescued the first two times, but I figured the drink would work eventually. I wondered what stopped me from doing it properly – jumping the gap, the bridge, leaping in front of a train – all the foolproof ways. But whenever I plucked up the courage to do it, an image of my uncle's face roared through my mind – right from nowhere – always laughing at me with that sideways sneering smile, shouting out, "I've won, I've won, I've won."

The only thing worse than this hellhole of an existence was knowing my bastard of an uncle had won.

When they finally figured it out, my parents did try and help. I saw at least ten counsellors, some ridiculous, one or two kind. I preferred the ridiculous, my feelings were safe with them. The kind ones stirred up all the filth, making the shameful feelings gurgle up past my heart where I could really feel them. Then it all became real.

I would never forget that one session when my feelings came so far up my chest I went into a fit, panting, hyperventilating, stiff in terror. I thought, 'this is it, I'm going to die.' I never went back to a counsellor after that one. Mary was her name. She would often make me draw. "This figure is you, Goliath; now colour in your feelings on the figure," or "draw a picture of your family, Goliath, it's okay to express how you feel. You've just got to find your own way to get it out. It's okay to express your rage, your shame." The word 'shame' undid me. How did she know? And rage, there was so much of it; so much nothing else would fit inside my body.

"Missing Margaret again?"

I had forgotten Fran was there, huddled next to me, looking out over the cold misty bright night.

"What exactly happened with Margaret, Golly? You never told me. We've known each other long enough now, haven't we?"

I glanced over.

"Piss off, Fran."

Fran turned and gave me her sternest glare. "I most certainly will not 'piss-off'! If you expect me to put up with your drinking and yelling and moping around, then it's about time you bloody well had it out, old man. Now what happened with that wife of yours?"

I had known the old witch for four years now and I'd never seen her so angry. I supposed she was right. I sat up in my bag, my back against the side of the chair next to her.

"Fair enough," I said and took a deep breath. Just the thought of telling someone made my throat seize up; but, somehow, I thought that counsellor Mary was right: the time had come to get it out.

"I was twenty-five. We were together for three years. Happy. Margaret was really talented. Cultured, she was, out of my league." I glanced over at Franny. "She was a pianist, you know. We'd go to the opera, to musicals, all the time."

Fran burst out laughing, hysterically; her high-pitched giggles echoed around the misty park. "You? At the opera – with all that long curly red hair and a crazy beard! What a sight!"

I waited for her to calm down. I think she sensed my anxiety because when she looked at my face, all tense and serious, her laughing stopped suddenly.

"I was very a different looking fellow back then."

"Alright then, Golly. Go on, go on," she said, her voice all serious again.

I took another breath and continued. "I'll never forget when I was twenty-eight. She took me to *Les Misérables*. It changed my life. The raw power of it. Those starving French revolutionists, slaves to the filthy rich, rising up against them to fight for their dignity and freedom. And Jean Valjean a basically good man – always on the run."

I could hear the powerful strains of the orchestra filling my mind. God how I'd identified with Jean Val Jean. Being on the run at least, I was not a good man.

"I cried the whole way through, actually cried."

"I've never seen you cry, Golly. Probably do you a lot of good."

"Don't you start." I didn't need another therapist.

"You know she brought me the music to *Les Mis*, and I learnt every song by heart. I actually have a great set of pipes."

Fran laughed again. "I don't doubt that for the screaming I

put up with. So how did you scare her off, you oaf? You weren't having nightmares then, were you?"

I turned away and couldn't answer. You see, it was Margaret's kindness, just like that counsellor; it undid me.

"One night she asked too many questions." I was whispering now. "Sweet Margaret, she was so tender, so close. It brought up all the shame. It was too, too much."

I turned and looked at Fran straight on, my throat so tight I could hardly make a sound. "I beat her. My beautiful Margaret. I beat her, Fran. Till her face was bloody."

I felt like throwing up and stared down at my feet, consumed with guilt and shame, hating myself with such an intensity my jaw went hard with rage. I remembered that night when I became that monster, just like my uncle. Her eyes had looked at me, so terrified, so betrayed, her tears flowing, her brow bleeding. It was that night I ran.

I haven't stopped running since.

Fran was quiet for a while. She was good that way, knowing when to speak. I was surprised by what she said next. "That was a real bad thing you did, Golly. A real, real bad thing. But I know you are not a bad person. I know that like I know the moon is alive, and the world full of magic."

I kept staring at my feet, my body all stiff and tight.

"You know what you need, old man?" She knew I was still young and often said this to tease me. Pausing, she looked at me intently, lowering her voice to a whisper. "Have you heard of Polops Point? A quiet spot no one knows of on the rocks overlooking the ocean at the south end of Queens Beach. It's along the Hermitage Walk, up the shoreline where all those rich wankers live in Vaucluse."

"What about it?"

"It's where old Ned died last April."

"So, I heard."

"There's something special there, Golly – something that puts an end to a man's madness. I don't know if it's white or black magic, but I know this place makes the measure of a man."

I couldn't help rolling my eyes. "Come on, Franny. White magic, black magic?"

"Didn't you ever wonder what happened to old Ned? A lot of blackness in his soul he had, a lot of bad things he'd done. He was not a good man. He met his maker at Polops Point."

"Ned died of a heart attack and you know it."

"There was far more to it than that." She lowered her voice again. "You have to believe me, Golly."

I shook my head.

"What about Ellen Ray?"

"Ellen who's all cleaned up?" I missed her company on the streets.

"She went to Pollops Point too."

"No surprise. She loves the ocean."

"She cleaned up the very next day."

"A nice coincidence."

"After fifteen years on the grog, and never missing a single day of drink? It's a big coincidence. And there's been others too. Mark me, Golly, there's been many who have never been the same since going to Pollops Point."

Franny waffled on a lot, but I'd never heard her talk all spooky and silly like this. The funny thing was her talk sent a clear chill up my spine. A chill of terror, a chill of wonder, and… something else. Something that made me want to go there. If for no other reason than for a trip to the water, just for something to ease my curiosity, to make me sit back and wonder what old Ned's last moments were like there, and what Ellen Ray's thoughts were that made her turn herself around.

A week later, late one night when Franny wasn't around to ask questions, I took the bus to Vaucluse and hopped off near Hermitage Walk. It was a still night, with not the slightest breeze, quiet as, and the moon was still bright, though only half full. Pollops Point jutted out onto a high secluded sheltered point surrounded by sandstone cave walls. Nestled between Milk and Queens Beach, it was almost impossible to get to through the trees and rocks, and at around 3am it was deserted.

I sat on the furthest point of rock and huddled against the cold, looking at the half moon, then down at the waves pounding against the rocks, and I wondered whether I was high enough to kill myself if I jumped.

On impulse I stood up and walked to the very edge of the cliff, placing my toes at the very tip. Just one step, one quick step would be all it took, and it would all be over.

I breathed deeply, mustering the courage to move my foot

over the edge, and like clockwork my uncle's face reared up in my mind, his laughter so real, his face so clear I thought that this time I'd really gone mad.

Perhaps he had died, and he had come back to haunt me? Perhaps there was something strange about this place after all? He laughter grew louder and louder, its sound pounding down on me, filling me shame, weakness, helplessness. I swayed and covered my ears, nearly collapsing and tripping over the edge…

And then, I heard it – the notes.

They were rising-up from deep down past my heart, rising from the very core of my soul, the notes of a song. I couldn't remember the name – was it 'When Tomorrow Comes' or 'Do You Hear the People Sing'? Whatever it was, it was a song from *Les Misérables*. It was Margaret's voice, it was Mary's voice, and most commanding of all – it was my voice, clear and pure, loud and strong.

It was the most powerful thing I had heard and felt in my life and it surged up into my throat, full and deep and loud; that song of the people who would not be slaves again, angry, vibrant, enraged, forceful, demanding their freedom, the orchestra victorious, determined, and loud.

And all that rage, which had sat stiffly inside me for so long, shot past my heart, came up through my throat and burst forth in a roar of sound and song for so long it felt like forever.

As the roar ended, I grabbed a small rock at my feet and took to my uncle' s sneering face, still laughing next to me; and

I pounded into his face, into the side of the cave, for what must have been ages – strong hard blows, until I was nothing but liquid roaring motion, and for the first time in my life I felt powerful. I was not harming anyone; I was just allowing all the feelings, all the energy inside that I'd shoved down deep, to rise up, and move in all its intensity with an honesty and a full awareness of my pain.

Eventually I found myself sobbing, deep-gulping gut-wrenching sobs; and when my tears were spent the sound of my uncle's laughter had gone with them, the image of his face was faded and changed. It was small now, pathetic, full of shame and hate and even fear. He was a man who had used his pain to torture and destroy another.

Then I saw Margaret's face, so hurt, so kind and beautiful; and I knew I had to fight for her, and even if she rejected me, or hated me and never wanted to speak to me again, I had to try. She deserved the truth at least. Tomorrow, I would go and find her. Just to talk.

There was so much to face, but I had a fire in my belly now, and my uncle was no longer a player in the game of my life.

I was free to live and fight.

About 'Do you Hear the People Sing'

'Do you Hear the People Sing' is a song from the musical *Les Misérables*. It is a powerful orchestral song at the climax of Act 1, expressing the will and determination of the French revolutionists uprising against the ruling oppressive rich. The power in the words captures the will and power that my character Goliath needs in order to face his past and start his life over, rather then be a slave to his shame. My story explores how unresolved emotional pain, or our 'shadow self', can be deeply destructive to others and ourselves; but when we have the courage to face it, we can start living our lives authentically.

Author: Sonia Zadro

Sonia Zadro is a clinical psychologist and freelance magazine writer who has written and published several short stories. Her story 'Oscar' gained highly commended in the 2016 BezerkaCon competition and was published in the anthology *A Fearsome Engine* (NBWG, 2016). Her stories 'The Big Dipper' and 'Bachorella' were published in various NBWG anthologies, and her stories '52 Hertz' and 'Yenali' were selected for inclusion in the 2019 and the 2020 Northern Beaches 'Art & Words Project', in the anthologies *Saltwater* and *Portrait* respectively.

Case 65726: The Lighthopper

Azmeena Kelly

How old am I? I no longer remember. It doesn't matter anyway, for my body remains forever frozen in the adolescent state it was in when they first took me away. It's only now, when I'm back in my original skin, that time can touch me; and I haven't worn this skin for a long, long time.

It has been many years since my last visit. Pillars of steel and glass have replaced the mounds of stone and earth, and the filth-encrusted lanes have given away to asphalt and sanitisation. The people look smarter, smell better; but I know that it would only take the smallest spark, a mere scratch to pull away the thin sheath of decency that keeps them from reverting back to the skull-bashing monsters still lurking beneath their painted faces. I have seen it happen often enough to know not to believe in appearances.

I'm not here by choice. I go wherever my masters send me, and if I don't comply, then I cease to exist. This time, they've sent me home.

This skin – my real skin, they tell me – feels alien in comparison to the slime-coated scales or the spineless blobs I have worn on other worlds. It looks normal enough, attractive by the standards I can remember concerning this time and place. But what I find discomforting are the feelings this body invokes in me. Senses that I had suppressed long ago have awoken again and distract me from the task my masters have given me. Hunger, lust, the warmth of sunlight on my skin, the delicious shiver down my spine at the hint of cologne on a passerby, I find myself constantly fighting against my own urges.

Maybe these feelings have lain dormant all the while this body was in the stasis chamber, waiting for me to inhabit it again. No one really knows if our bodies are capable of holding on to memories and feelings, or whether the body remains an empty husk until it is animated with life by a soul essence.

The smell of fried fat and sugar brings my attention back to the grease-stained paper bag on my lap. I pull out another sugar-coated ball of fried dough and bite into its soft centre. A sticky sweet red liquid the colour of fresh blood runs down my chin. Not a lot of the real me remains, and even this outwardly normal body comes with its modifications to help me do my job. But they can't stop me from taking my small pleasures where I can have them.

I'm watching a Lighthopper, a fugitive from another place who is hiding inside a human. Seeking refuge within a host isn't illegal per se, for there are other creatures harbouring within hosts, with permission. But this creature is hitching a ride without consent, and this creature is resisting its return to the Source, which cannot be allowed.

It is hiding inside a girl child and, from the level of integration with its host, it likely embedded itself at the time of the child's birth. To the girl and her mother, nothing would seem out of the ordinary, and any odd behaviours would politely be put down to an active imagination. Lighthoppers are very good at hiding.

The girl has been doing what she did most mornings. She and her mother would have walked to the park with their dog around the same time each day, and the child and her dog would have played, her mother sitting on the grass while checking her phone or reading a book.

This morning the child is throwing the dog a stick, which it retrieves by running as fast as its stumpy little legs will carry it. It drags the stick back along the grass to the girl; then stands, quivering, until she throws the stick out again for it to fetch. They've done this routine every morning, though neither child nor dog ever seem to tire of the game.

The dog runs over occasionally to sniff my hand, and today I give it a scratch behind its ear, as I have in the past. The child then runs after him and hovers nearby, as she's done in the past. I am now a regular here, and sit on the same bench every day to watch them.

"Hello, Isabella."

"Hi, Val," she says, bursting into a smile. The dog is pulling at the stick in her hand.

The girl's mother has always kept a close eye on her child. This morning she's chatting with another young mother who's walking her baby through the park. She catches my gaze and gives me a small smile, reassured by the fact that the stranger whom her child is talking to is a pretty young woman with a blooming belly of her own. And the dog seems to like me too, which is reassurance enough that her child is safe.

The girl throws the stick into the middle of the park, much farther than a child her age should be able to; then she pulls herself up onto the bench next to me. Her eyes drop to the crumpled up bag in my lap.

I don't want to share the last few bites of my treasures, as I know it's going to be a long time before I'm able to experience them again. However, I pass the bag over to her and can't help but smile as she snatches it out of my hand.

"Hasn't your mother taught you any manners?" I ask, raising my eyebrows.

The girl looks up at me, her eyes wide, and for the briefest instant I catch sight of the creature that I'm hunting.

To anyone else, it would have looked like nothing more than a reflection of light crossing over the girl's eye. But I know what it is. A Lighthopper, an energetic parasite. I can't tell which species it is, or its origins. I'll only be able to see its true form once I extract it from the child. The girl looks back down as she shoves the remaining morsels into her mouth, smearing powdered sugar over her face and hair.

"Thank you," she coughs through a mouthful of pastry.

"Do you know who you are?" I ask.

The girl nods as she chews, then stops. She seems to stop breathing.

Then, just as suddenly, her body shivers all over for an instant, and she awakes as if from a trance.

"Do you know who you are?" she asks in a singsong voice.

I watch a frown of confusion cross her face as the Lighthopper speaks through her. Her true self seems to realise that something is wrong.

"You know who I am." I grab a strand of my hair to twist around my finger as I speak. "I'm here to take you back to the Source."

The girl turns her big brown saucers of eyes to look up at me.

"You don't have to," she says slowly. "Maybe you could pretend that you didn't find me?"

I stop playing with my hair and put my hand on her arm. "You know that's not possible."

The dog returns with its stick and, this time, instead of throwing the stick back at it, the girl stoops down to pick up her pet. It squirms in her too-small lap, twisting side-to-side to lick powdered sugar off her hands and face.

"I have a name here," she says. "A mother who loves me and who has given me a name. And I have Tiger."

The dog barks at the sound of its name, scrabbling off her lap and running off after a butterfly.

"And I need to take you home," I sigh.

"My mother won't let you take me," she tries, as her voice becomes shaky.

"She's not your mother, and if she knew who you really were, she would run screaming to her god for help ridding herself of you."

The girl shakes her head, her ponytail flicking across her ears.

"Can't you tell them someone else beat you to it? That I was already gone when you got here?" she whines, her eyes filling up with fat little tears.

"It doesn't work like that; you know that." I shake my head.

"But what harm will come from me being here? I just want a chance to have a life. I am a lifeform, so why am I not allowed to live?"

"You know why you can't. You don't belong here. You're an anomaly, and all the while you remain, your presence saps time and energy from this world into wherever it is that you've come from." I turn to look at her, at the innocent brown eyes staring up with me with the unreadable expression of a four-year-old child.

I sigh. "You need to understand that the longer you stay here, the more you endanger everyone and everything you love in this place."

"But you're here," she tries to rationalise. "Why can you be here and not cause time to get sucked into a hole?"

"Because I am from here, originally… And, because I no longer exist in the same sense that other lifeforms do."

I pick up my cold coffee, take a sip, and purse my lips before pouring it onto the grass. "It's time for you to go back."

"But if I go back I will die," she says, her voice wavering. "And Isabella – this body – will die. She needs me to live."

"She may; she may not. She is not my concern. You are," I whisper. I don't like how a lump of guilt is forming in my throat. "And you are already dead."

The girl jumps off the seat and stands to face me. "You can't make me go. I'm not afraid of you!" she shouts, turning and running away.

I watch her run to the mother, who scoops her up into her arms. She starts to walk toward me, a surprised and scornful face aimed right at me; but the girl screams and shakes her head so much, the woman turns and carries the child home, the dog pulling against its lead in its haste to lead the way.

Isabella and her mother live near the park, within one row of identical ivory terraces set along a narrow street, canopied with dark-leaved oak trees so tall they blot out the sun. Their neighbours are Mrs Tan and her teenage twins, Ari and Phoebe; and Mr Balta on the other side. Mr Balta struggles to get up and down the stairs and relies on Isabella's mother to help him with his chores. I know about them all now, and feel like they know me too.

The cracked pavement along the street bubbles with tree roots attempting to push their way through the concrete, some managing to penetrate here and there. I walk as slowly as I can, stopping in front of my favourite trunk to savour the feel of its smooth bark against my hand, one last time. I don't know if this tree, or if any of these trees will still be here the next time they permit me to come back.

I have spent countless years hardening myself to the point that I do often forget that I was human once. Yet in less than two weeks within this body, I have become as soft and weak as I was when they first took me. My mission should have been over by now, and the longer I've lingered, the more difficult this has become. But my task cannot be put off any longer.

I'm in front of the house, fighting the urge to run away as a sense of dread overwhelms my senses. Through the front gate I can see a pink-tasselled child's bicycle leaning against the porch, its pink and white straw basket squished onto the ground. A plastic black-haired doll, the kind designed by toy makers to clinch young children's instincts and sympathies, pokes its head out of the basket and stares up at me with big painted eyes.

Just then, from the neighbour's open window, I catch the middle of a song, an older rock song warning about a higher power, and the lyrics resonate in my mind. I take a deep breath to calm my twisting stomach, then push against the gate. Its rusty lock snaps easily under my fingers and I walk to the front door.

This is easy. I've done this a hundred times before, I tell myself.

But I no longer believe it as the sound of my heart thumping in my chest drowns out my footsteps.

I knock on the door three times. Inside the house, I can hear the thudding of small feet followed by a barrage of sharp barks, followed by another set of heavier feet coming down the stairs.

"Mummy, no!" Isabella cries to her mother.

Then there's silence.

I knock again.

A muffled voice calls to Isabella. "It's alright, darling," the mother reassures her child. "It's just the postman."

I wish it was just the postman. Why though? I'd done this so many times before.

The mother's voice draws near as she moves towards the door.

"No, Mummy, no!" Isabella stamps up the stairs.

The mother runs up after her.

I turn the knob and step into the house.

Tiger is standing by the door. He wags his tail when he sees me and drops down onto his haunches.

"Sorry buddy, no treats this time," I say with a small smile. I like Tiger, but I have a job to do and there can be no witnesses, not even the almost sentient.

"Tiger!" Isabella's voice screams from the upper floor.

"Good dog." I crouch down and hold out my hand for Tiger to lick one last time. The dog moves toward me and stops, letting out a small whine.

"I'm sorry," I whisper as I pull out the small collection vessel from my pocket, along with my knife. "Go in peace, little one."

A pale stream of light flows out of the dog's still-open eyes, and starts to stream upwards towards the Source. I hold the collection vessel above the light stream to capture it, and the dog's life energy moves into the tiny container, big enough to store the soul of the small animal.

I tuck the vessel now containing Tiger's soul back into my pocket and stand back up.

The hallway opens up into a living area, where a television is playing an advertisement showing a car full of laughing school children eating burgers. In the kitchen, a saucepan of pasta sauce bubbles unchecked, splattering the white bench top with bright red dots. Beyond the living area is a small outdoor courtyard, cluttered with potted plants and more toys.

I walk slowly up the stairs, shaking my head to clear this irrational feeling of dread inside me. It's this body, I tell myself. There's no other explanation for this irrational hesitation.

"Leave us alone!" The mother stands in the doorway of a room at the top of the stairs, her face wet with tears. "I've called the police, they'll be here any minute."

Peeking out from behind her legs is the child, in a yellow and pink polka-dot dress. She grips a battered brown bear tightly in one hand.

I pull out another collection vessel.

"Isabella," I say, "it's time to go, home."

About 'Case 65726: The Lighthopper'

My inspiration for this story was 'Sympathy For the Devil' by the Rolling Stones. It makes me think of a character who has been around for a long time, who can move through time, and is present at various events throughout history. My character normally doesn't get attached to the places she has to visit, but this time she has been sent back home to Earth, and she's reminded once again how it feels to be human. It's been a long time since she was last here, and even though the place no longer looks like it once did, it still feels like home.

Author: Azmeena Kelly

Azmeena Kelly writes speculative fiction based on human interactions with technology and artificial intelligence, and imagines realities where science and magic merge into one. Azmeena has published a number of short stories online, in anthologies published by the Northern Beaches Writers Group, and is working on her first novel, which began its life as part of a novel-writing course though the Penguin Random House Writers' Academy. Azmeena has a professional background in science, law and change management, and lives on the Northern Beaches of Sydney with her husband, two children and two cats.

The Search

Tara Ray

For the first few months after our arrival in the Florida Keys, I don't do much of anything. I sit in cafés and watch the tourists. I loiter in gardens and sketch the plants and flowers and insects. One day I am so absorbed in drawing the trees and clouds, I forget to cover my bare shoulders, which turn pink and freckle under the bright sun. When he comes home that evening, Carlos approaches me as I cook our supper and kisses my sunburned shoulders.

"You ought to wear sunscreen," he whispers into my neck.

"Maybe," I say, turning to face him and return his kiss. "Or maybe I'll let the sun bake me until I'm a shrivelled old raisin. Will you still love me then?"

"I'd still love you if you were as shrivelled as a raisin or any other delicious little piece of fruit."

"Who are you calling little?" I ask. Even in my bare feet, I'm tall enough to look down at Carlos' head. I kiss a newly exposed patch of skin along his receding hairline. "And I'll love you when you are as bald as a golf ball."

He looks up at me. "How's The Search?"

I shrug.

The Search is what we're calling these months of my unemployment. I've saved enough to allow for a few months of soul searching, an attempt to figure out what to do next for work. My special snowflake thing, something that makes me shine. Because clearly my previous forays into retail and interior design were not 'it'. There has to be more to life, more to *me*. Our move to Florida for Carlos' new job felt like the ideal opportunity for a fresh start.

After Carlos leaves for work the next day, I swipe a bold shade of coral across my lips before walking the two blocks to the market. As I apply my makeup, U2's song 'I Still Haven't Found What I'm Looking For' plays on the radio and I sing along.

I slow as I pass a tattoo parlour with the name 'Black Heart' emblazoned in white across a black awning. I don't remember having seen the place before. Every inch of wall is covered with illustrations. I assume these are the images on offer, so that prospective clients can select the design they want sketched on their bodies. The doors to the studio are open, allowing the sound of music and the gentle hum of the tattoo machine to spill from the shop. At the sound of the machine, I try to peer inside, unable to resist my curiosity. The person being tattooed has their back to the street, while the tattoo artist leans over their wrist in concentration. The design in progress is too small to see from my perch in the doorway.

Another day later that week, I return home from the market, my bags heavy with papaya and plantains, and stop dead in my tracks. The *Black Heart* door is once again open. A woman lies face down on a table. The artist is hunched over her, making intricate black marks across the woman's back.

The tattoo is huge, spanning her entire torso from the base of her spine to the nape of her neck. The delicate black lines twirl and spin along her back, reaching like fingers toward her dark hair. From time to time, the tattoo artist leans back and tugs absently on a large silver earring. As he appraises his work, he glances up to see me loitering in the doorway. He raises an eyebrow, then resumes his work. A few minutes later, he sets down the needle and rests one large, heavily tattooed hand on the woman's arm. "I think that's enough for today. We'll finish the rest next time."

The woman sits up and, as she reaches for her top, I have a full view of her back. She pulls her blouse gingerly over her shoulders and begins to button it. She turns toward me.

"Sorry," I say. "I didn't mean to stare. It's beautiful. Your tattoo, I mean. I've never seen anything like it. Did it hurt?"

"A little. But it's a good kind of hurt," she chuckles, her voice low and husky. "But the credit for this beauty goes to him." She gestures toward the artist who is cleaning his instruments.

"You're very good," I say to him. "Your images are extraordinary."

"You know about tattoos?" he asks.

"No, not all. I sketch a little just for fun. But I don't know about tattoos."

"You gonna get one?" He sweeps his arm toward the selection of images covering the walls.

"Me? No. I mean, no thank you."

He gives me a long look. "You just here as a spectator then?"

"I guess so. Sorry. But that design on her back… I've never seen anything quite like that before."

"Well, if you change your mind, you know where to find me."

I nod and walk home.

Several of my friends have tattoos, but I've never been attracted to them before now. Each design here is unique. Even sketched on paper, they breathe and glisten. I want to touch them, to feel their pulse.

Each morning on my walk, I linger in the door of the tattoo parlour for a little too long.

One morning, when he doesn't have any customers, the artist calls to me. "Want to get a closer look?"

I step inside, set down my bag from the market and approach the sketches that line every inch of the walls. In addition to designs, are photos of finished tattoos. I lean in closer to the images. His pen and paper sketches are excellent, but his designs are even better on skin. He has a knack for adapting them so that the curves and colours blend seamlessly into the body. Once etched on a human canvas, his designs truly come to life.

"You really are talented," I say.

He grunts something that sounds like 'thanks', followed by, "You said you sketch too?"

"A little. But I'm not really trained or anything. It's just something I do for fun."

"You think I studied at the Sorbonne?" He snorts. "Lots of us are self-taught. School of Life is best, that's what I say. You got any drawings with you?"

I hesitate before pulling a sketchpad from my bag. "Like I said, it's just something I do for fun." I hold the pad out to him. I rarely let anyone else see my sketches. It feels too intimate.

The artist takes my pad and sits in one of the chairs. He puts on a pair of reading glasses before stooping over my designs. I watch as he turns the pages. He inspects them for a long time without saying anything. At last, he closes the sketchpad and looks up at me. "I don't think I've introduced myself. My name's Ed."

"Hannah," I say, extending my hand.

Ed shakes it and looks at me carefully.

"You're very talented, Hannah." He hands me back the sketchpad. "Lots of people, they think they're artists. All it takes is a pen and paper and they think they can draw. But you're actually good. What do you do?"

"I'm not working at the moment. My husband and I moved down here together and I haven't started working yet."

"You ever thought about doing this?" Ed gestures around the parlour. "Being a tattoo artist? It's not the most glamorous job in the world, but it's not bad. There's something about seeing your art literally come to life, you know? Like you imagine something, then it walks out of here on someone's arm or leg or back or whatever."

I turn away from him for a moment, and run my fingers along one of Ed's designs, imaging I can feel the flesh rise beneath it. "When can I start?"

Ed laughs. "Hey, now. I don't think I offered you a job, exactly, did I? Just asked if you had thought about it. I've got a hunch that you'd be a natural." He rubs his chin and gives me an appraising look. "If you'd be willing to help me out around the shop, maybe with the cleaning and that sort of thing, I could try teaching you."

The next day, I am waiting outside *Black Heart* when it opens. Ed rolls his eyes when he sees me.

"I said you could spend some time here. Not that you needed to be here the very second we're open."

"I'm excited."

"I gathered that."

Once inside the shop, Ed tosses me a rag and hands me a spray bottle. "How about you get started with the windows."

"I feel like the kid at the beginning of Karate Kid and you're Mr Miyagi."

Ed rolls his eyes again.

Later that day, when the windows are washed and the floors are sparkling, Ed beckons me over while he tattoos a tiny turtle on the ankle of a young woman. I hover nearby, wanting to watch but not interfere. U2's 'I Still Haven't Found What I'm Looking For' plays over the shop's speakers and Ed hums along. I wonder if I *have* finally found what I'm looking for.

"I just heard this song the other day," I say.

Nobody responds.

After the woman leaves, Ed says, "Did you know my brother is a surgeon?"

"Um, no. I didn't."

"People are surprised to hear that sometimes – both of us growing up in the same fancy-pants Californian suburb but ending up so different. My parents are so damn proud of him and think I'm just a bum slacker living down here."

I open my mouth to object but Ed raises a hand to stop me.

"No, it's okay. I'm happy with how things turned out. Wouldn't have it any other way. Anyway, my brother, the surgeon, he told me the way they do it is 'see one, do one, teach one.' I reckon that will work for tattoos too. So you start by watching. Pull over a chair and watch the next one I do. If it's okay with the customer, I'll talk you through what I'm doing."

I watch intently as Ed tattoos the next customer. After he leaves, Ed says, "I guess it's your turn now."

"Oh, I really don't think…"

Ed reaches into his backpack, pulls out an orange, and tosses it to me. "You can start with this."

I catch the orange and look down at it. "What's this for?"

"You're gonna give that orange a nice tat. You can choose the design, but start with something simple. I'll walk you through it."

With Ed's guidance, I hold the orange in one hand and the tattoo machine in the other. At first I press too hard, squirting myself in the face with juice. Before long, I understand the right pressure to apply.

"That's right. You're getting the hang of it," Ed says.

After lunch, I return to the shop with a basketful of fruit. I tattoo oranges, grapefruit and papayas. It feels very different from sketching on paper, but I love it.

"Okay," Ed says. "Now you teach one. Walk me through what you're doing."

This time Ed holds an orange in his hand as I instruct him, step by step. When he is finished, he shakes my hand. "Congratulations, I believe you're almost ready to graduate to people. Tomorrow you do one on me."

"On you? You want me to do my first tattoo on you?"

"Well, who else is it going to be? You've inked an entire fruit basket. I think you've got the idea. But I sure as hell am not going to let you learn on a customer. You might mess it up your first time."

"What if I mess it up on you?"

Ed shrugs. "Only one way to find out."

I gather the fruit I used for practice, wondering if they are still safe to eat. As I pack them into a bag to carry home, I stop and stare. Didn't I draw a fish on an orange and a tree on the papaya? Now the flesh of the orange appears untouched, and a fish sits near the base of the tree. I rifle through the other fruit. I clearly remember drawing a bird, and it's not here at all. Confused, I shove everything into the bag and hurry out of the shop.

The next morning Ed pushes up his sleeve, revealing more of his heavily tattooed arm. He scans his skin and points at a small uninked patch of flesh, roughly ten centimetres in diameter. "How about here? Why don't you give me something small right here?"

"What should I do?"

Ed shrugs. "Oh, I don't know. I don't care really. As you can see, this ain't my first rodeo. But give me something original. I'm tired of all my own designs," he says, nodding his head in the direction of the sketch-laden wall.

"What do you like? I mean, other than tattoos."

Ed considers this for a moment. "I like women. Beer. And the ocean. I love the ocean."

I pull out my sketch pad, start a few designs, abandon them, and begin again. At last, I complete one and place the drawing in front of Ed. "What about this?"

Ed looks down at my drawing of a small mermaid. She is simple but somehow both delicate and bold. Ed smiles. "That's perfect. Give me that. If you can translate that drawing onto my arm, I'll be mighty impressed. Give it a shot."

I'm so nervous I'm afraid my hands will shake and I'll ruin it. I close my eyes a few seconds and imagine a giant bubble of calm sliding over my head until it envelops my entire body. I see myself stepping into it, serene and safe. I've come so far. I have run, crawled, and scaled city walls. I open my eyes and my hands are steady. Very gently, I hold one hand against Ed's arm as I begin to tattoo him with the other. Ed doesn't watch as I work; he keeps his eyes focused somewhere in the distance. For that I am grateful. As I finish, I pull away from him and inspect the result with satisfaction.

"There," I say. "Take a look. What do you think?"

Ed looks down at his arm and his face breaks into a wide grin.

"Damn, girl. I think you're going to put me out of business if you keep this up. I don't think I've ever seen such a natural. If that's what you can do your first time out of the gates – just wait."

I smile. "I'm glad you like it."

"It's awesome. People are going to love you."

As we stare at the mermaid, the tip of her tail flicks.

My eyes dart to meet Ed's. "How did you do that?"

"I didn't do anything."

"But you saw it, right?"

Ed nods, wide-eyed. As we stare at the mermaid, she tilts her head and smiles at us.

I pull back and look at Ed, whose jaw has dropped.

"Oh my god," he mutters.

"That's not possible," I say.

"Do another," Ed demands, as he frantically scans his arms for available skin. He pulls up his shirt and points to his stomach. "Here. Do another one here."

"I don't think that's a good…"

"Just do something else," Ed demands.

I hesitate, then nod. "What should I do?"

"I don't care, anything."

I sketch a few designs in my notebook and hold it up for Ed.

"All of them. Do them all."

"Are you sure?"

"Positive."

I try not to look at the mermaid. I think she's doing hula moves with her arms and the sight of her makes my stomach turn. I lean over Ed and tattoo image after image onto his skin. I force myself to focus only on the image I'm working on and ignore the others. When I finish, I lean back and Ed bends forward to look. A silhouette of a woman arches her back and stretches her arms above her head. A tree's branches sway in the wind. A fish swims in the empty space between the other designs. Ed and I gasp in unison as a bird flaps its wings, flies to the horizon of Ed's belly, then disappears.

Ed blows out his cheeks and grins. "This is going to be huge, Hannah. We're going to make a fortune with this. You're going to be famous, girl."

"But I don't understand… how is this possible?"

"Who cares? It's amazing. The most incredible thing I've ever seen. We'll have people lining up out the door. But no birds, okay? People will want their money back if their tats leave."

"But why would someone want this?" I say, gesturing at the images swimming and squirming on Ed's skin. "It's… unnatural."

Ed frowns at me. "None of this is natural. Tattoos are not natural."

"But don't people want tattoos so they have something permanent?"

"No, they want to be different. They want to feel unique."

I lean back and shake my head. "I have to go," I say.

"Now?"

I nod and start gathering my things. I try not to look at Ed's stomach, even though he still hasn't pulled down his shirt. I think the woman just winked at me. I recoil.

"Come in early tomorrow, okay? We've got a lot of planning to do. This is going to be huge," Ed says again.

I don't answer as I rush to the door. I begin my journey home at a rapid clip, though as I continue my footsteps slow. I feel oddly hollow. Something doesn't feel right.

All I want is distance between me and those… *things* I put on Ed's body. The very idea of those moving images is disconcerting. I don't understand how it's even possible. The lack of predictability frightens me. Here I thought I was the creator, yet I never expected to imbue my creations with a life of their own.

They shouldn't be moving at all – the fact that they are feels confusing and wrong. I think of those images moving of their own accord, and I imagine their colours bleeding together, into one monstrous shape.

Monsters, that's what they are – and they must never be again.

By the time I open our front door I've decided – I won't be going back. I won't see Ed again; I won't tattoo someone again.

So, what then? Haven't I been looking for something like this to set me apart?

At the kitchen table, I rest my head in my hands and resolve to keep going, to keep searching. Tomorrow. Tomorrow I will walk in the other direction. I will walk away from *Black Heart* and discover what lies in the opposite direction. There are so many neighbourhoods, so many places, there must be something else.

Like the song says, I'm not exactly certain what I'm looking for, but I feel sure now: I'll know when I find it.

About 'The Search'

Back in 2014, Joshua Rothman, a writer for *The New Yorker*, wrote that U2's 'I Still Haven't Found What I'm Looking For' is "a song that celebrates wanting." Rothman explained that to him "the most interesting thing about [the song] is that you *don't* find it. It's about the search." This is the feeling I wanted to capture in my short story – that hunting for something elusive and just out of reach. I wanted to focus on my character Hannah's search for a sense of meaning that remains indefinable and beyond her grasp.

Author: Tara Ray

While Tara Ray has a background in public health, she has interwoven her love of language with her interest in improving community health throughout her career. She has co-authored several academic papers and spoken at national conferences in the U.S. This is her second story to be included in a Northern Beaches Writers' Group anthology. She also had short stories selected for inclusion in the Northern Beaches 'Art & Words Project' in 2019 and 2020, in the anthologies *Saltwater* and *Portrait*.

Song For A Moment In Time

Susan Steggall

Vee leant over the railing of the *Radar*, watching the jade green water swirl past the hull of the old ferry. Thinking again about a recent meeting she'd had with her boss made tears of frustration well up in her eyes and flow into the general saltiness of Sydney Harbour. She fumbled in her handbag for a tissue.

"Are you alright?" asked a woman standing nearby.

"Yes, thank you. I'm fine."

But Vee wasn't fine. If she didn't write a decent piece for her next assignment as a freelance arts reporter, she would probably be passed over for future jobs and the bills were piling up.

"What about some artworks in the Biennale? Something *different*, Vera Agnes," her boss had insisted, using her full name, which he only did when he was displeased with her.

Vee had never been comfortable with her name; it was so old-fashioned. Could it be the reason she often felt she didn't fit in – to the art scene, or anywhere in the contemporary world for that matter? Although she was not really interested in the past, preferring to drift in the present, she occasionally wondered where 'Vera-Agnes' had come from. The only reference she had was an inscription 'From Mary to Vera-Agnes' in age-worn letters on an old hipflask – a rare family heirloom.

After that awkward meeting with her boss, and its subtle insinuations of failure, Vee had returned home determined to make a start on her assignment. Instead of consulting art magazines for information about the Biennale, her eyes had strayed to her mother's diary. It had lain unread for almost a year since her sudden death at the age of seventy. Vee had flipped through its pages, hoping for clues. Among accounts of domestic days and holiday highlights, there had been one entry about a grandfather who'd been raised in a foster family.

"I knew him well," Vee's mother had once said. "You look a bit like him. It's your dark blue eyes." Vee had asked for more information, but her mother had merely shrugged and said, "it's all in the past."

When researching family members, one usually starts by consulting great aunts, distant relatives and the like, but Vee's family was pitifully small. She had one brother and one cousin, and when asked, both had said they'd never heard of a Vera-Agnes. Vee's father had arrived in Australia as a 'ten-pound Pom' in the migrant drive after World War II and cut all ties with his previous existence. A possible mystery there, but one for another time.

Vee had decided to visit Sydney's Mitchell Library to look up nineteenth-century immigration records. She found a Vera-Agnes, born around 1855, who had arrived in Sydney with her family in 1865. There were no details as to whether this Vera-Agnes might be related to Vee, but it was a start.

Arriving home tired from her searching, Vee had slumped into a chair and turned on the evening news. Halfway through an interview with the curator of the Biennale of Sydney exhibition, an image appeared on the screen of an industrial building filled with curving white sails. It was on Cockatoo Island; Vee sat forward. When the curator started talking about the island's convict past, and subsequent site as a correctional centre for orphaned youths and wayward girls, Vee gave it her full attention.

"Might be worth a visit – and an article," Vee said to her marmalade cat.

Head bowed, still thinking about the meeting with her boss, a loud blast from a merchant navy ship made Vee look up to see her ferry had passed into the western reaches of Sydney Harbour. Up ahead, Cockatoo Island looked like a squashed broad-brimmed hat. Flat foreshores surrounded a high central 'crown' topped with buildings, water towers and the spreading canopies of Moreton Bay fig trees. To the south the hat's 'brim' disappeared under a jumble of roofs and huge cranes thrusting skywards.

The *Radar* rumbled to a stop. Vee disembarked and paused to take in her surroundings. The mix of architecture – from convict era to mid-twentieth century, in buildings of honey sandstone, red brick and metal – held the island in a time warp, its penal and industrial pasts, including its important role in repairing ships during World War II, now subsumed under contemporary tourism.

A volunteer Biennale guide handed her a map and pointed to a barn-like building where Vee confronted larger-than-life portraits of first Australians with piercing, unsettling eyes. In a brick and timber warehouse she watched a video installation of animated charcoal drawings. At the Turbine Shop a female voice filled the cathedral-like space with a haunting song – 'The Internationale', according to the plaque on the wall. The original lyrics, composed by Frenchman Eugene Pottier, were a rallying cry for workers in the 1871 Paris Commune. Here on Cockatoo Island, the song was a plea for freedom and tolerance.

Vee continued her art tour, but no other Biennale work moved her quite like that anthem. It wasn't exactly the words, although these were stirring enough – *uniting the human race, standing unbowed, taking destiny into one's own hands* – it was the slightly hoarse, untutored voice of the singer echo-ing around the huge disused building, embracing generations of men and women who had suffered at the hands of oppressors.

Unites the human race…

With the words ringing in her ears, Vee took the steep steps at the eastern end of the island. She climbed past tree roots clinging to the vertical escarpment, roots as thick as elephants' trunks. At the top, she followed signs to the convict precinct on the western end of the plateau – a complex of weathered sandstone dormitories, officers' quarters, gaol and roofless military guardhouse.

Vee sat on a wooden bench on the edge of a gravelled courtyard. As her eyelids began to droop in the warm afternoon air, she sensed someone watching her, but when she opened her eyes she was alone. She had never believed in ghosts, yet there was something about the histories embedded in the sandstone that invited the imagination to roam free. Vee closed her eyes again, willing whatever or whoever to reappear. At the sound of light footsteps Vee opened her eyes. Just as a young woman wearing a long brown dress under a dirty apron reached out a hand, a stern voice interrupted.

"Ma'am you have to leave, now. You've fifteen minutes to make the last ferry. Otherwise…"

Imagining herself locked in a prison cell for the night, Vee scrambled to her feet and hurried after the ranger. On the return trip to Circular Quay she could not get the incident out of her mind: had she seen a ghostly spirit or merely imagined one? Maybe time travel did exist – parallel universes and all that.

At the earliest opportunity, Vee set out for Cockatoo Island again. She dressed in jeans and sneakers, packed a rucksack with water, snacks, torch, phone and, as an afterthought, the old silver hipflask filled with brandy. She rubbed her fingers over the family treasure, its delicate tracery worn smooth by the years.

As soon as Vee disembarked, she headed for the plateau to search for a hiding place well away from the prying authority of the rangers. All the buildings were locked or barred by wire fences except for those in which Biennale artworks were displayed. Near the remains of grain storage silos cut into the rock face, she found a door ajar at the base of a derelict corrugated iron building and stepped inside. It was an office and although dust had settled a grey sheen over everything, it looked as if its occupants had only recently left their posts. Shelves were piled with logbooks, workmen's overalls hung on hooks and a bulky manual typewriter sat on a wooden desk that had a generous space underneath.

She memorised the location and continued walking, inspecting every nook and alleyway. As the sun was sinking in the western sky, the foolhardiness of what she planned to do almost overwhelmed her. She could barely breathe, and beads of sweat were trickling down her forehead. 'Madness,' whispered reason, though a different voice in her head repeated 'now or never', over and over, like a drumbeat. She hurried to hide under the desk until darkness fell. Once judging it safe to come out, she made her way to the convict quarter to sit on the same wooden seat.

It wasn't long before she heard a rustling sound as a slight figure in the same shabby dress appeared in a patch of moonlight.

"Who are you?" Vee asked calmly although her heart was pounding.

"I was about to ask you the same question. My name is Vera-Agnes…"

"That's my name too. Friends call me Vee."

"You dress funny. Where're you from?"

"Your future, I think."

The young woman's face showed disbelief. "When in the future?"

"2008," Vee replied. "I'll tell you about me but first I'd like to hear your story. What year is it?"

"Could be 1878 or maybe 1879. It's difficult to keep track of time here." Vera-Agnes eyed Vee with suspicion. She circled the courtyard, checking doorways and corners, before beginning to speak. "I sailed from England to New South Wales with my grandmother, my parents and three young 'uns. From Sydney we went by paddle steamer to Newcastle where my father found work on a farm. It was a good life, for a while." Her face fell.

When she began talking again it was in a sad small voice. "It was around 1868 when a group of men set out for the Victorian Gold Rush, my father among them. He didn't find gold, but he didn't come home either. Mother took in washing, and I helped at the local inn, but it wasn't enough."

A sharp screeching sound erupted from a large tree beyond the courtyard. Vera-Agnes looked as if she were about to flee.

"It's probably an owl. Don't go. Please continue," Vee entreated.

"Let's walk." Vera-Agnes flicked her head for Vee to follow. "That's where we sleep," she said, pointing to a long building.

In daylight Vee knew it was empty except for rows of rusty iron bed frames, but in this otherworld time, she could see silent figures of young women fetching and carrying. She had to shake herself to concentrate as Vera-Agnes began talking again.

"Mum got sick with the coughing disease and died. Grandma

Mary took in lodgers. I went to work at the big house up the road. I fell in with a gang of pickpockets. I was caught and sent to a school for wayward girls. Then all of us from Newcastle were moved here to Cockatoo Island. *The Biloela Reformatory*, it's called." Vera-Agnes kicked at a stick. "*Biloela*'s supposed to be an Aboriginal word for Black Cockatoo. Black prison'd be more like it."

"It doesn't look much," Vee said, the words of 'The Internationale' reverberating in her head… *the rights of the poor* – a hollow phrase… where was equality?

"No better than the old place," Vera-Agnes replied. "We were promised schooling to 'reform' us but there's been precious little of that, just backbreaking work. We're often punished, even for things we haven't done. One time the superintendent decided it was me who'd drawn on the walls of the dining-room. He told me to rub it out. I said I wouldn't 'cause I hadn't done it. He kicked me and pushed me over. I got this when I hit my head on the floor."

Vera-Agnes pulled her hair back to reveal a jagged scar across her forehead.

"That's terrible," Vee exclaimed. "He'd no right to do that."

"It's us that have no rights," Vera-Agnes replied. She walked to the edge of the plateau and pointed to the silhouette of a large ship docked just off the island. "It arrived a few years ago to serve as a home for neglected boys. We weren't supposed to mix with them, but it was easy to get through the fences and meet the lads." Vera-Agnes smiled. "That's how I met Tom. He was smart and hard working. We planned to run away and make a new life for ourselves…" she paused, as if searching for words.

"When the authorities found out I was in the family way, Tom was banished to a loggers' camp somewhere up north and I never saw him again. I was sent to the reform school at Watsons Bay. That's where I had the baby. I called him Thomas…"

"My brother's name," Vee whispered. "Keep going."

"The midwife let me hold him for a while. She said he'd go to a good home and, if I liked, I could give him something to remember me by. The only decent thing I owned was my grandmother's *flashkitt* so I hid it in his bundle of clothes." Vera Agnes gave a sob. "That was the last time I saw my Thomas. Then I was brought back here."

"That must have been very hard on you," Vee said softly.

"I don't matter. I keep wondering what happened to my baby."

"I'm sure he'd have been alright." Vee got out her phone to make a note of everything Vera-Agnes had said.

"What's that?" Vera-Agnes asked, a frightened look on her face.

"It's a telephone – for talking to people. It does other things too."

"What do you do, in that future of yours?" Vera-Agnes interrupted.

"I write about art – or at least I try to."

"Wish I'd learned to read and write. Maybe you could write my story?"

"Maybe I could," Vee nodded. They leant on a fence in

companionable silence for several minutes. Vera-Agnes began humming softly under her breath… *if only I could free my spirit from its prison…*

"How do you know that song?" Vee asked.

"It's in the island. I think it's singing to me."

Suddenly a terrible commotion broke out: shouting, banging and sounds of wood splintering.

"Gotta go," Vera-Agnes exclaimed. "If they find I'm missing there'll be hell to pay." She turned and ran.

Vee hurried to her hiding place. In the darkness she tripped over a rock and sprawled headfirst onto the path. She sat up and turned on her torch to find blood oozing from a gash on her leg and one ankle swelling rapidly.

After a while she tried to stand up, but her foot gave way. "Mustn't panic," she gasped.

"No, you mustn't," a familiar voice replied. "It's me – Vera Agnes. I've come to see if you are alright. Hard to find you, though. This place looks real different all of a sudden. That's the super's house over there, but what are these other strange buildings?" Once again she looked about to take flight.

"They're after your time," Vee replied, in as soothing a voice as she could manage. "They're in mine, in the future. A lot has happened in the way we communicate with each other – even in my lifetime."

Vera-Agnes acknowledged this with a grunt and inspected Vee's foot.

"I'll help you, but I can't take you back to my place. There's been trouble. We're copping it." She was speaking as if in pain herself. Vee shone the torch over her and was horrified to see a huge purple bruise on the other woman's face.

"Never mind me," Vera-Agnes said, putting a hand to her swollen eye. "I'm used to it."

She fished a strip of cloth out of her pocket and tore several broad hairy leaves off a plant growing nearby. "This should do the trick. Comfrey." She placed the leaves on the cut and then gently bound Vee's swollen ankle. "You'll be alright here even if a bit uncomfortable."

Vee got out the brandy flask, took a sip and offered Vera-Agnes some.

"Mmm that's good. Nice *flashkitt*." She turned it over in her hands, ran her fingers over the engraved sections. An angry expression flared on her face. "But this is mine! Where'd you get it? My grandma gave it to me. It was supposed to go with my baby."

Before Vee could explain it was a keepsake handed down through *her* family, Vera-Agnes clasped the flask tightly to her chest, well out of Vee's reach.

"Nice meetin' you. Must go before I'm missed." She touched Vee's hand before disappearing into the night.

In the morning Vee inspected her foot. There was barely a trace of the cut and the swelling had almost disappeared. Had she imagined the whole thing? Been delirious? Was it a dream? As Vee stood up a slash of white caught her eye. It was a strip of calico stained with dried blood. Remembering Vera-Agnes tearing leaves off a plant, Vee looked around and found several bare stems. The hipflask was nowhere to be seen.

There was no sign of any disturbance at the convict buildings when Vee went to check. She waited on the plateau until several ferries had disgorged their passengers, then descended to the lower section of the island and walked towards the wharf. As she passed the Turbine Shop, the strains of 'The Internationale' mingled with the cool salty breeze. *No rights… no rights…* resounded in her brain.

Determined to find Vera-Agnes' son, Thomas, Vee searched registers of Births, Deaths and Marriages and spent more hours in the Mitchell Library poring over old newspapers and Benevolent Society records. When the last pieces of the puzzle fell into place, Vee sat for many minutes, overwhelmed by sadness for Vera-Agnes mixed with elation that now she knew her family's story.

On her third visit to Cockatoo Island, Vee headed straight for the convict quarters, sat in the same spot and waited; but the magic had disappeared. In desperation, as closing time loomed, with head bowed, she began to speak.

"Thomas was taken into a family who lived in a village north of Sydney. In 1890 he married Adeline and they had two children: William and Harriet. William was killed in a terrible war in France. Harriet married and had two daughters – Wynn and Jean, my mother. Thomas died in the 1940s so he never met me, his great-granddaughter."

She paused, choosing her words carefully. "Vera-Agnes, please know I'm proud to have met you in this extraordinary connection across time." Vee waited, her ears straining to hear footsteps, her nerves stretched to breaking point. She was about to leave when she felt a calloused hand on her arm.

"You can't see me no more. My spirit is fading but I heard every word. Thank you for the story of my Thomas. I can leave now, knowing he had a good life."

A current of air brushed Vee's face and a faint 'clink' resounded on the stone next to where she was sitting.

"I've brought you the *flashkitt*," came so softly on the breeze that Vee thought she might have been imagining it. At her feet was the silver hipflask.

Vee felt a lightness in her heart, an unfamiliar sense of optimism. She had no idea, yet, how she could write Vera Agnes into an article about an artwork on Cockatoo Island but knew that, somehow, she had to – something about history as singing, sculpture in sound. As she walked to the ferry wharf, the strains of 'The Internationale' floated across the balmy afternoon air. Yet it wasn't the voice of the well-known artist she could hear but the sound of Vera-Agnes humming the song of the Turbine Shop.

In a soft voice Vee began to sing: *We have been naught, we shall be all…. We'll change forthwith…* The words of 'The Internationale' would forever now be linked to a girl from long-ago, on an island.

About 'Song For A Moment In Time'

I became fascinated by the unique industrial environment of Cockatoo Island on a visit to the 2008 Biennale of Sydney exhibition. The theme – 'Revolution: Forms That Turn' – was evoked in artworks that expressed a desire for change and a need to alter perspectives.

In the Turbine Shop the untutored voice of Scottish sound artist Susan Philipsz filled the cathedral-like space with a haunting version of 'The Internationale', composed as a rallying cry for workers in the 1871 Paris Commune. Ever since I have wanted to link the island and the power of that song in a story about a woman at a crossroads in her life.

Author: Susan Steggall

Susan Steggall's publications include *Alpine Beach: A Family Adventure* (1999); novels, *Forget Me Not* (2006), *It Happened Tomorrow* (2013), *'Tis the Doing Not the Deed* (2019) and *The Heritage You Leave Behind* (2021); art-related articles; exhibition and book reviews (in print and online); and book chapters. *A Most Generous Scholar: Joan Ker. Art and Architectural Historian* (2012) was a Non-Fiction winner in the 2013 Society of Women Writers NSW Inc (SWW) Book Awards.

Susan has edited anthologies for SWW and the Independent Scholars Association of Australia Inc. She is a keen member of the Northern Beaches Writers Group and her short stories 'A

Poetical Science' and 'Away with the Fairies', were published in the anthologies *A Fearsome Engine* (2016) and *Of Beasts & Butterflies* (2019).

The Air You Get

Zena Shapter

Vicky checked her appearance in her smartphone's inset video screen, guided her long auburn hair to drape over a shoulder, then pulled at her age lines. The larger screen was still black, its 'poor connection' message gleaming white in the centre. She had a moment to refocus. When Lauren came back online, she wanted to look and sound her best. Her two sisters, Lauren and Kaia, were all she had right now; and with them living on the other side of the world, she couldn't risk upsetting either of them – not when she'd already upset Rob.

She tilted her face into the late afternoon sun. Its glare hid the dark circles under her eyes. Behind her in the garden, palm leaves rustled and the hairy orange claws of a kangaroo paw knocked about in a cooling breeze. It was the perfect backdrop.

She would miss the garden if they had to leave.

"Can you hear me?" Lauren's voice. The screen filled with her image. London's dull morning light paled her face. Eight years younger, Lauren didn't have age lines – though it had been so long since they'd seen each other in person, Vicky couldn't be sure. The screen bounced as Lauren walked to her 8am thyroid appointment. Her short-cropped hair shone coppery in places. "What was it you were saying about breathing?"

"Um," Vicky remembered, "that Yoga teaches all different kinds of breathing – awareness breathing, segmented breathing, we can work with ratios, breathe from our bellies or chests. There's an advanced workshop I want to take, in case the virus spikes again in Australia. It could really help people."

"Damn it, I forgot to call Kaia again – I've been so busy with the move."

"She's okay." Vicky resisted adding 'now'. Kaia lived in Sweden and her family had just struggled through Covid-19. But what had been a two-day flu for her husband and their boys, had been a five-day drowning for Kaia. At its worst, Kaia had fled to the hospital, scared and panicked. 'I can't breathe,' she'd texted Vicky one night. 'I can't breathe!' Vicky had been petrified. But Kaia was better now and Lauren didn't need to know the details. As Rob had pointed out yesterday, people had enough problems without Vicky adding to them. "Did you know," she said instead, "in Sweden they only test if you're in a risk category?"

"So how did they know she had it?"

"Symptoms. The doctor came out to her car, tested her oxygen levels – said she was fine to ride it out at home. Apparently, the worst part is the panic. You're breathing and breathing but just can't pull enough oxygen into your lungs; your body thinks you're dying and starts shutting down. Staying calm can mean the difference between life and death."

"Sounds like *everyone* needs to take that workshop!" Kaia exclaimed.

"I know, right? And so many of my clients have asthma or allergies."

"So things are going well then, teaching yoga?"

"I have such amazing students." Vicky left out the part about having only ten, split between two weekly classes, both online. "I'm teaching soon actually."

"No graphic design work?"

Vicky shook her head, pretending not to care so Lauren wouldn't worry. The jewellers where Rob worked as an accountant had closed down. No more job for him, no casual design work for her. The financial pressure was almost too much to bear – scrutinising figures every day, applying for mortgage breaks, cancelling memberships, assessing and reassessing responsibility for their lack of savings. If only Vicky had accepted the full-time graphic design position she'd been offered last year, rather than continuing to train as a yoga teacher.

But when Vicky had finally admitted as much yesterday, Rob had thrown his hands up and walked out the room, muttering, "as if I haven't got enough problems."

They hadn't spoken since.

"Well, yoga suits you." Lauren turned a corner and frowned.

"You okay?"

"Still getting my bearings. Hey, at least I'm outside!" Lauren pushed her shoulders back and dragged down a deep breath. She had been in isolation for two weeks, following her arrival in

England from Prague – no friends, no family. Another new job, new city, and a boss who wanted her at work days ago. Now Lauren's thyroid was playing up. Enough problems. "And Rob?" Lauren asked. "You two okay?"

"Better." Vicky's throat stuck on the lie. "Has been since 'The Big Yoga Talk' last year, when I turned down that job. He honestly didn't realise how unhappy I was doing graphic design." That part was true. "He knows now that he's seen me teaching. Even comes to classes." Though only to make her appear popular until more regular clients signed up.

"So, no more 'yoga is stupid'?" Lauren mimicked Rob's voice.

"No." Vicky chuckled awkwardly. "He knows we all need to live our own authentic lives. I'd support him if he wanted to pursue his." If they weren't divorced by then. She should probably dig up some kangaroo paw to take with her…

"And the kids?"

"Good. Impressive, actually. Online learning set them back, but…"

The screen juddered, shadowed. A thud, then blackness.

Had Lauren dropped her phone?

"Stop!" Lauren screamed. "Stop!"

"Lauren?"

"Help!" Lauren yelled, her voice fading. "Stop!"

A man in a black beanie appeared on a funny angle, scarf wrapped around his nose and mouth. He strolled along the street, no Lauren in sight.

Strolled?

No Lauren?

"Hey!" Vicky shouted into her phone. "Where's my sister!"

The man glanced down, then disconnected the call.

Fingers shaking, Vicky called Lauren's phone. It went to message. "No, no, no!"

A sweaty Rob hurried onto the garden deck, trowel in hand – he'd been clearing a blocked stormwater drain. "Is it Kaia?"

"No – someone attacked Lauren!"

"What?"

"A man stole her phone. She could be hurt!" Vicky blinked back tears, opened an internet browser and searched for how to call UK emergency services from overseas. She found the number for London's Metropolitan Police and dialled.

A pre-recorded voice said she was seventh in the queue.

Her heart pounded. "Lauren could be dead before they answer!"

"Try Crime Stoppers?" Rob rubbed her back, his callused touch as warm and gentle as when Kaia had texted about not being able to breathe.

More precious minutes of internet-searching, dialling, then an excruciatingly long phone menu to select the right option. A pre-recorded voice reported a forty-five minute wait.

Rob hurried inside, returned with his phone. "Stay on hold, I'll call triple-zero, see what they can do."

"Yes," a female operator told them, "we can ask the Met to drive by. What street was your sister on?"

Vicky's throat tightened. "I don't know."

"Her home address?"

"I only know the suburb."

"Can you get it?"

Vicky had the phone number of the shared house Lauren had rented in Prague, and for various friends there. "I'll try." What else could she do?

But most of Lauren's friends were still asleep. She had to call several times before they answered.

Minutes nudged into an hour. No one had her new address. The triple-zero operator called back – police had driven around the suburb's main streets but Lauren hadn't been found.

Tears resurged, quickly cooling on Vicky's face. The afternoon sun had dropped into a hoary grey dusk; the air chilled. She was scheduled to teach yoga soon. How? Her eyes were red. Her sister was missing and could be hurt. "First Kaia, now Lauren," she sobbed, her voice trembling.

"Vicky, stop." Rob sat cross-legged in front of her. "What is it you say in class? Let go of what you can't control, save your strength and energy for what you can. You couldn't help Kaia when she was sick; you've done everything you can to help Lauren now. You can't control who gets hurt."

"I know." And the reality of that was terrifying. "Why do you think I'm shaking?"

Rob took her hands. "Just take a breath and pay attention to the life around you. Breathing is a gift – isn't that what you've been studying? Breathe and be grateful for the air you get."

The same words she'd told everyone last class. She'd even

played a sitar version of The Hollies' track 'The Air That I Breathe' to put everyone at ease.

She closed her eyes and inhaled slowly. Her lungs shuddered but the air felt good. It always did. Crisp. Cleansing. Focus on it, nothing else. Just breathe. The expansion reached into her. She exhaled and drew down another. This time when she released the air she felt calmer. Slightly. Breathing was the only thing she could control. A few more breaths, then she opened her eyes.

Rob smiled, his blue eyes brightening as she gazed back. Was that pride in his expression?

Suddenly, her phone beep-beeped.

Lauren, calling through a social media site. Her beautiful face appeared onscreen. Safe. Unharmed. She was on her laptop at home. "Oh my god, can you believe that guy – bloody thief!"

"Lauren? You're okay?"

"Sprained my ankle when he pushed me over, had to hobble to my appointment. Got a massive cut on my head too." Lauren lifted up her fringe to reveal a bruised gash. "At least my phone was backed up in the cloud. And I made it home in time for that video conference with my boss."

"But," Vicky stammered, "but that man, he *strolled* away from you. I… I thought you were dead."

"Dead? I ran after him, threw rocks, even a shoe; just couldn't keep up with his bike."

"His… bike?" The man must have been pedalling, not strolling.

"Yeah. Wasn't the phone pointing right at me? I thought

you saw all that, otherwise I would've called you sooner. Sorry, sis."

"I only saw his face. I thought…"

"That I was dead?" Lauren laughed. "Geez, sis, I know coronavirus has us all stressed out, but maybe it's you who needs to take a breath? Listen, can we talk more later? I need to file a police report before I forget what he looks like. I'm sorry you thought I was… dead! Love to Rob and the kids!" She blew a kiss then ended the call.

"She's okay." Vicky sighed in relief. "She's okay."

"She is." Rob was still sitting cross-legged on the floor, calm and patient.

Vicky frowned. Rob had quoted her yoga teachings? He knew about her studies? "I thought you said yoga was stupid?"

He stood with a huff, stomped towards the deck's steps; then stopped and turned. "That was *one* comment," he snapped, "over a year ago. Why do you have to keep bringing it up?"

"*I* keep bringing it up?"

"Yes, and I don't know why – you're the only one bloody earning right now! Who cares about a year-old job offer you didn't even want?" He tutted, then closed his eyes, rolled his shoulders and took a deep breath from his belly, expanding his chest like in class.

So… he *didn't* blame her for their finances?

Rob opened his eyes. "Vicky, the way you've diversified into online classes, advertised and found the clients you have – all I can do is dig up the garden! And you *are* helping people. Look at me, I was about to stomp off – I didn't thanks to your bloody yoga!" He smiled and opened up his arms. "Hug?"

Vicky stood, tears building though there were none left to shed. She hadn't meant to upset anyone. With all their money worries, maybe the stress *was* getting to her?

"I'm sorry for snapping," Rob wrapped his arms around her. "It's so hard being out of work. Your classes really help." He loosened his hold. "Come on, time for you to help more people, and get paid for it!"

He stepped away but she clung on a moment. She needed it to sink in – her sisters were both alright, and… maybe she and Rob were too?

It's you who needs to take a breath, Lauren had said.

"Rob?" Vicky murmured, then paused. What did she want to ask? Whether they were going to be okay? Whether teaching yoga would earn enough to see them through? He gave her a squeeze, and she knew – the Hollies were right: all she needed was the air that she breathed… and to love Rob. He was here. She was here. The kangaroo paw wasn't going anywhere. Things weren't perfect, more stressful times no doubt lay ahead, but right now she had to get changed for class – to help him, to help others, to learn herself: how to breathe.

So she straightened and drew down what precious air she could, along with the fresh scents of dirt clods on Rob's clothes, the pungent sweat on his skin. There was only one thing left to say. "You'd better get changed too."

About 'The Air You Get'

My story was inspired by The Hollies' track 'The Air That I Breathe', the lyrics of which remind us that all we really need in life is the air we breathe and love. Following the coronavirus pandemic, this inspired me to write a story about misconceptions and dealing with stress. My character Vicky experiences this with both Rob's unemployment and Lauren's phone theft, though it's the phone theft that enables her to see more clearly that her stress is getting to her, causing her to imagine extremes. Thus, in the end, she realises the same might be true of her relationship with Rob. When I heard 'The Air That I Breathe' on the radio, I realised that the answer to Vicky's stress is right in front of her: in the breathing exercises she teaches in her yoga classes. All she needs to do – all any of us need to do when we're stressed – is to take things one step at a time, breathe and be grateful for the air we get. Thank you, The Hollies, for your words of wisdom!

Author: Zena Shapter

Zena Shapter writes from a castle in a flying city hidden by a thundercloud. Author of *Towards White* (IFWG 2017) and co-author of *Into Tordon* (MidnightSun 2016), she's won over a dozen writing competitions – including a Ditmar Award, Glen Miles Short Story Prize, and Australasian Horror Writers' Association Award for Short Fiction. Her short stories have appeared in the Hugo-nominated *Sci Phi Journal, Midnight*

Echo and their Australian Shadows Awarded 'best' anthology, *Antipodean SF*, and *Award-Winning Australian Writing* (twice). She's a movie buff, story nerd, writing mentor and editor, book creator, short story judge and an inclusive creativity advocate, who's founded community creativity projects for writers such as the 'Art & Words Project' and the award-winning Northern Beaches Writers' Group. She loves frogs, chocolate, potatoes, and travelling. Find her online via social media @ZenaShapter and zenashapter.com

Hotel Coolangatta

Kate Mitchell

The balmy Queensland breeze hit me as soon as I'd retrieved my check-in luggage from the carousel and stepped through the sliding doors. I pulled off the jacket that I'd been so comfortable in only three hours ago on a nippy Melbourne morning, and stuffed it into my suitcase. The queue at the taxi stand was only two deep, so I headed over.

Everything was flowing nicely. No need to be anxious, I told myself.

I took three soothing breaths and scrunched up my hair. It was a fruitless exercise, given that the plane air had rendered my normally bouncy curls limp.

I checked the time and took my phone off flight mode.

"Hotel Coolangatta, please," I said to 'Barry' as he shoved my suitcase in the boot.

He grunted in acknowledgement.

I was relieved he turned out to be a man of few words; I wouldn't have coped with another chatty man like Wu, the Uber driver who'd taken me to the airport that morning. I now knew Wu's entire life story.

It had been sixteen years since I'd been to Coolangatta. How different I had been then. Early twenties, footloose and fancy-free. Like the party would never end.

I sighed and tipped my head back, staring up at the ceiling of the cab. If only I could go back in time, with this brain. I would invest in Google or a house or something and not be in the predicament I found myself now.

I looked out the window at the glittering ocean of Kirra Beach as we cruised along Musgrave Street.

'Hotel California' started playing on the radio. I smiled and closed my eyes. No other song had the power to transport me back to my childhood in New Zealand as viscerally as this Eagles' song did. I remembered listening to it while sitting on the back bench seat of our orange Kingswood Holden. The sun had heated up the vinyl seat so much that Dad had to place a towel under my bare three-year-old legs so they wouldn't burn. I remembered looking down at my round tummy, my 'puku', in the tight blue togs with colourful polka dots, and feeling the constriction of the black seat belt across my body. I liked to chew on that seat belt. Black seat belts always tasted the saltiest.

Something else tugged at the edges of my memory. Like an unhappy toddler pulling on his mother's skirt.

"Here," said Barry, snapping me out of the trance.

Hotel Coolangatta was on the eastern side of Boundary Street, a street divided down the middle by two states. The eastern side was Queensland. I thought of my friend, Tash, who used to live in Tweed Heads, New South Wales, though worked in Currumbin, north of the border. During daylight savings she would have all the clocks in her house kept on Queensland time so she wouldn't be an hour late for work.

Butterflies returned to my gut. I could do this. I had to do this. I'd done it before.

I briefly considered the 240,000 Australian women aged 55 or older at risk of homelessness. I shook my head. I had to think positively. There were two months left until Christmas. Next year – 2020 – was going to be my year. I still had time to turn my ship around.

I squared my shoulders and got out of the cab, 'Hotel California' still playing on the jukebox in my mind.

I paid Barry and proceeded up the ramp to the hotel, wheeling my suitcase behind me.

Hotel Coolangatta was typical of its kind in the area – tropical, yet slightly run-down and seedy looking. There was always an air of seediness about the Gold Coast.

I pushed the glass door through to the reception area and gave the receptionist my name.

"Two people booked in for tonight?" she asked, frowning into her computer monitor.

"Yes," I said quickly. "Um, he'll be arriving later."

Either the receptionist had a great poker face, or she was used to arrangements like this.

"Third floor. Enjoy your stay," she said, handing me the plastic key card.

I entered the lift with trepidation, checked my phone and figured I had a good hour to get settled in before…

"Hold the lift!"

A young couple bumbled in.

"Thanks – we're on the tenth floor, don't fancy taking the stairs!" the girl explained, her wide smile showing perfect white teeth.

I smiled back and watched them surreptitiously in the lift mirrors. The boy had curly black hair and caramel skin, and was playing with a strand of the girl's long blonde beachy hair and staring straight into her eyes as she chatted about their afternoon plans. It was such an intimate, affectionate act, I had to look away. They seemed so carefree and happy. I looked at my own reflection. Had I ever been loved like that? I saw an old and burdened woman staring back. Thirty-nine years old, divorced, no money, no kids. What was the point of… me? I felt like I'd taken a wrong turn in life and was now hurtling towards eternal misery.

The lift arrived at the third floor. I stepped out, leaving the couple in their loved-up cocoon.

I let myself into room 303 with my plastic key card and braced myself for the slightly smoky, mouldy smell that always accompanied these kinds of rooms. I was pleasantly surprised. The room smelled faintly of pine-scented cleaning products and salty sea air. There was even a small balcony – and a view! Maybe tonight wouldn't be so bad after all.

I had a quick shower and made a cup of tea, then sat out on the balcony to drink.

My stomach grumbled, reminding me it was time for lunch. But I still felt too uneasy to eat. I was always nervous with clients I hadn't met before. Because you just didn't know did you? What they would be into? How would they look? How was their personal hygiene? I shuddered at an unpleasant memory. But this one was paying me well. So, there was that.

I watched a group of kids playing on the beach and cast my eyes further north to the skyrise horizon that was Surfers Paradise. A cockatoo squawked suddenly, making me jump.

There was a knock at the door.

I headed back in, hastily throwing my cup into the sink and checking my appearance in the mirror as I walked past the open bathroom door. I still had a pretty good figure for my age. I was conscious that, while I couldn't hold back the wrinkles on my face, I could try to keep my body in good nick.

There was another knock. I smoothed down my bright pink kaftan.

"Coming!"

My mouth felt dry as I peeked through the peephole. The man looked nice. Better than nice, in fact – he was a full-blown hottie! He was tanned, bald with a shaved head. Like a young Kelly Slater.

I suddenly felt excited and self-conscious all at once. Would he be disappointed? My photos were recent and not some filtered version from ten years ago. Surely, he knew what to expect?

"Who is it?" I called, waiting for the correct code name.

"Mick," he replied.

I exhaled, not realising I'd been holding my breath, and unlocked the door.

"Come in, Mick," I said, with an air of false confidence. I was the one in charge here.

"Hi," Mick said, extending his hand. I held my hand out to shake his, but he grabbed my wrist and kissed it, taking in every inch of my body with his warm chocolate eyes. This might be fun, I thought.

I giggled and pulled him over to the couch.

"Okay, first things first, I need to run through the usual points upfront, your expectations, my boundaries, safe words, that sort of thing…" I was struggling to keep my composure and suddenly felt vulnerable. I would never get used to this line of work. It rattled me that Mick was so young and gorgeous. He could pull any woman he wanted! Why did he book me?

We talked for another few minutes as I finished up with my usual procedures.

"Okay," I said, brightly, "start on the bed?"

Mick nodded.

We both jumped at a sudden loud bang on the door.

"Mick! Mick! What are you doing?! I know you're in there!"

"Oh shit," Mick's face paled.

"Who is it?" I asked.

"My ex." Mick rubbed his head and sighed. "I'm not cheating on my girlfriend, if that's what you're thinking."

"Who am I to judge?" I said evenly, although the thought had crossed my mind. It wasn't uncommon in my profession.

"Mick! Get out here right now!"

The woman's voice was shrill, her knocking frantic.

"You better…" I started.

"Yeah."

I hid behind the bathroom door, peered through the gap at its hinge, and watched Mick unlock the door to the bedroom.

"Nicole, what the hell?"

"Who are you with?!" Nicole demanded. She tried to barge her way in, but Mick stopped the door with his foot and put his arm across the gap.

"You know you're supposed to stay away from me!" Mick was angry now.

"I saw your car! What are you doing…?"

"Nicole, you need to leave before I call the…"

"No! Mick, no!"

Nicole gave one big push and I watched in horror as Mick cried out in pain and crumpled to the floor.

"Where are you, bitch?" Nicole called out, stepping over Mick and looking around the room.

My heart leapt out of my chest – she was holding a knife in her right hand! There was blood on it!

No, no, no, no, please God, no, I prayed. What the hell was happening?

I slammed shut the bathroom door and leaned all my weight against it. No lock?! My breathing was ragged and shallow, I felt close to collapsing.

"Nicole, please!" Mick's muffled voice.

There was a thump on the other side of the bathroom door. Then another.

Nicole was throwing herself against the door.

"Stop!" I shouted, tears running down my face. "Just stop!"

She wasn't going to stop. I knew that. I glanced around for something I could use as a weapon. The only thing I could reach was a hairdryer. I ripped it off the wall, then opened the door to retaliate. Everything moves in slow motion.

Mick on the floor. Anguish etched across his face.

Nicole and her crazed green eyes. Trails of mascara down her cheeks.

The hairdryer raised high.

My legs giving way, falling, falling.

The bright red stain blooming across my hot pink kaftan.

I could hear Don Henley's grainy voice. I remembered being three years old and sitting in the burning bench seat of our orange Kingswood Holden. Dad in the driver's seat, turning the radio up.

"Neat – 'Hotel California' – love this song, bunny."

Me happy, but hot and impatient to go to the beach. Wearing my blue polka dot togs. Waiting for my mum and baby brother James.

The black seat belt.

I loved chewing on black seat belts. They always tasted salty and made me think of fish and chips.

Dad swivelling around in his seat, "yuck, don't put that in your mouth."

Dad pulling the salty black seatbelt out of my mouth.

Dad's foot slipping off the brake.

The orange Kingswood Holden rolling down our steep driveway.

Mum stepping out of the house with baby James on her hip.

I could feel the pain now. The searing stab in my abdomen triggering the repressed moment that had changed my life's trajectory.

Why did I chew on the black seatbelt? It was all my fault. It was all my fault!

I choked and made a guttural sound, then everything went dark.

My legs were burning in the back seat of our orange car. The towel under me was too small. The cicadas were noisy. Daddy was turning up the radio.

"Neat – 'Hotel California' – love this song, bunny."

I felt happy, but hot. I wanted to go to the beach and Mummy and James were taking ages!

My puku was round, like a ball, in my tight blue togs with the rainbow dots.

I stroked my black seat belt. I loved chewing on black seat belts. They always tasted salty like fish and chips.

A wisp of memory floated in my mind, like a soft white feather.

I did not feel like eating fish and chips today.

"Plenty of doom at the Hotel Coolangatta!" I sang.

Daddy burst out laughing. "Beautiful singing!" He smiled at me in the rear vision mirror.

Mummy opened the back door and plonked James in beside me, tucked into his bassinette.

"Ready for the beach?" she said.

I was.

About 'Hotel Coolangatta'

Sometimes it can take only a few bars of a song to transport me back in time. The song 'Hotel California' by the Eagles does this for me most vividly. The memory in this story of the song playing on the radio in the orange Kingswood Holden is completely true, minus the tragedy! So, it got me thinking: imagine if certain songs had the power to create time-travel portals. Then I remembered Nietzsche's Eternal Recurrence theory of living the same life over and over again – but what if you kept going until you got it right? The protagonist in this story is unhappy and regretful. She feels like she took a wrong turn somewhere, which transpires to be the insignificant act of chewing on a seatbelt as a child. It's true that often the smallest acts can have the power to change the entire course of your life. But it's a hopeful thought that maybe, just maybe, we get infinite chances to get things right.

Author: Kate Mitchell

Kate has been passionate about writing and illustrating since time immemorial, but only recently decided to share her creations with the world. Her first short story was published in 2020, in an anthology for the Northern Beaches 'Art & Words Project', *Portrait*. Outside of her day job as an insurance underwriter, Kate works on her copywriting business, in addition to working on her children's picture books, a commercial fiction novel and a self-help book. She has completed three writing courses with the Australian Writers' Centre and feels indisposed if she hasn't drawn for a couple of days or is reading fewer than six different books concurrently.

Honey Coming Back

Peter Fagan

Talia clenches her jaw and studies her reflection in the car mirror. She breathes a soft sigh of relief, safe in the knowledge that nobody around here knows her. She's dishevelled and sporting a hooded jumper, even though it's balmy North Coast weather. The hoodie offers up the impression of earthiness: the perfect antithesis to her careerist self. It makes her appear defiant, fully elevated into that other world. Or maybe the depth of her rage has transformed her from careerist to vigilante, and her clothes are now the embodiment of the avenger?

She strokes her bicep against the backdrop of a morning breeze creeping through the driver's window, carrying the scents of lush green countryside and rolling hills. Must be all this training, she muses. For weeks now she's been immersed in regimented cardio sessions; they help her focus and maintain her motivation against the demons she needs to quell. Her body is firm and she's feeling on edge; like she's ready to anticipate and disable any threat. She turns up the music; it helps heighten the mood, puts her in the zone. She's only twenty minutes away from the farm. Come too far to turn back now.

As she nears its gate, the farmer is already waiting for her. She fidgets in her jacket for her purse. Seconds tick away as she rustles. Keep your identity cards concealed when your purse opens, she tells herself. She listens for anyone approaching from the shed behind him. Since she last spoke to him, the farmer hasn't shown any signs of over inquisitiveness, beyond listening to her concocted tale of struggling to fend off wild turkeys ravaging her orchard. Things need to stay that way.

She turns her eyes towards the skies. The wind is howling now and the trees surrounding the farmhouse shake. This has got to work. In truth, an orchard is about the last thing she owns. She *owns* crippling debt and the remnants of a relationship with an ex-boyfriend now sucking her dry.

"Here you go." She holds out two hundred-dollar bills.

The farmer takes it, then delicately transposes the agreed quantity of 240 milligrams of Strychnine from a transparent canister through a funnel into a silver hip flask. "Now keep the hip flask well away from any personal stuff. Any loose drop will stain clothing. Rat on me and… I'll find ya."

Talia snorts and a smirk creeps across her face. She fixes him with a glare and pauses.

"Rat on me and… I'll fuckin' kill you."

She swallows involuntarily and turns the car around.

The streets of Lismore border on desertion. There's a hurricane warning ten days old. The same warning was issued twice before Christmas and once in January, all of which were averted. But this week McCluskey notices a distinct uneasiness in the streets. Heads are low and the locals all march purposefully from the shops to their cars.

McCluskey is unperturbed by this conspicuous urban desertion as he drives through the main street. Maybe nobody is coming through the Northern Rivers with a drug quantity of any sizeable proportion *this* weekend, but he remains hopeful. Operation Nettle is eleven months in progress. Just one more bust under his belt and he'll be one step closer to making justifiable noises about a 'successful' Operation Nettle. He'll be out front and centre when the State Commissioner announces statistics showing a drastically reduced illicit drug trade on the North Coast. Then he'll be within touching distance of a willing ear in the Federal Police Drugs and Customs Division. Means a move back to Sydney.

He presses his lips with steely determination and thinks about where he could relocate the family. Botany maybe or Cronulla? Close to decent schools, the coast; ocean swimming, the good life.

He slows to an intersection three kilometres from town and gets ready to barricade one side of the highway.

—○—

Douglas James paces backwards and forwards, ruminating over

the same tattered carpet in his shed as he has for the past five minutes. He knows he must follow up with McCluskey. He tells himself he's only doing what anyone facing jail would do. He casts his eye out of the shed and to his nearest barn. On last count, the whole farm of near 100 hectares was devalued by 40%, thanks to China going elsewhere for wheat. The publicity hasn't helped either: his appetite for twenty-something European flesh landed him in quite a hole. The backpacker he hired as a farm labourer willingly climbed a ladder to paint the main residence. He says he guided her down the last few metres by helpfully placing his hand on her hips. She disagreed and wasted no time in launching a police complaint.

Can't buy her off now, even if he could afford to. Seemingly she's back in Finland, but on standby for a righteous tirade at court. Last week, the lawyers informed him the court in Sydney was only too willing to accommodate her giving evidence via audio-visual link.

He closes his eyes momentarily. Going to prison, he'd lose the farm. Nobody would step in. Well, nobody he could trust.

But there's still room for a good ending, he tells himself. He can still avoid a custodial sentence and, just maybe, the whole saga evaporates – if McCluskey is as good as his word.

He lowers his head to his phone and lets out a deep sigh. He's promised him *something* tangible, don't have much this week – except for her.

"Better not be fuckin' with me, Doug." McCluskey gives Doug a chance to supplement his information. It's not the best. "That's it? Poison? No green crop transactions? You've plenty to lose here, mate." He listens as Doug recounts the vehicle and driver description: young woman, mid-thirties, dark skin, brown hair, and not a local according to Doug. He says he put the poison in a hip flask for her. McCluskey nods his head at the mention of a hip flask – in a moving vehicle it could justify a stop and search. It's just the damn wind outside he fears. Clouds darken and multiply by the minute.

Talia allows her eyes to drift momentarily to the left: Lismore 37. Her elbows tremble as she struggles to grip the steering wheel, traversing at only 30 kilometres per hour on a standard two-lane 80 zone highway. Only 37 kilometres to go. But the howling wind is intensifying. A weather warning alert illuminates her phone screen, in the middle of the passenger seat. For the past two hours, the radio station signal has been interrupted by flash flood alerts and warnings that hurricane winds are expected to intensify over the next four hours. She had to turn them off, switch on a CD. But now roadside signs to the right and left are buckling. The car shakes violently.

She clenches her teeth. At this speed she has, what, fifty more minutes before she reaches Lismore? Then she'll get a cheap hotel room for the night.

The wind outside whistles ominously. She's all too aware she is taking a risk now, with every telephone line ahead besieged under the strain of the storm's savagery. Her thoughts quickly turn to a recent conversation with a friend, who witnessed telephone lines crashing onto roads and killing motorists.

Guatemala, was it?

Not sure. She slows to a snail's pace; she can't see beyond 15 metres now. Either side of the highway hedges are blowing over, almost horizontal. Pulling over isn't an option. The roads will be impassable soon and she's facing possible death in a wild hurricane if she's stuck outside. Sooner or later the police will divert all traffic and block entrances to Lismore centre. Time to think about options – what will she do if they stop her?

Can't lie – the street cameras in Nimbin would confirm she was there.

Shit. If the police search the car… Even the dumbest, most naïve cop on the country beat is not going to believe her: driving alone, into and quickly out of the epicentre of Australia's thriving marijuana industry on the same day, then back to Sydney. Not exactly an inconspicuous tourist.

Sure, they don't bust you in Nimbin; that dents the local economy. They wait until you're 50 kilometres away; then bust you.

Just how the fuck do I explain what I'm doing up here, 600 kilometres from Sydney? No relations in the area, definitely no friends. Work?

Douglas, that farmer? I could pretend I work for him, I could call him now?

But I'm the furthest thing from a farmer. And him pretending to the police that I'm in his employ, on an errand, in a storm?

She glances at her bag on the floor of the passenger seat. Playing high stakes now with 200-odd milligrams of deadly Strychnine poison. The plan she'd hatched now seems like the dumbest revenge plan anyone could dream up. She could've snuck in and knifed Jeff in the back during one of his romp sessions at the whorehouse. It would have been dark in there and the reception is usually empty. She could have knocked over any dumb bitches in the way.

Talia shakes her head ruefully.

Why didn't I just buy a bottle of perfume, empty it and swap in the poison? I'm looking at jail-time before I even land a blow on Jeff. The headlines? Jesus Christ.

Mother of toddler caught with poison, driving in a deadly storm, having left her son 700 kilometres away. Apprehended close to the marijuana epicentre of Australia. Buckles under questioning and admits to a conceited plan to poison her ex to get sole custody of her son.

Just 20 kilometres now to Lismore and any cheap motel for the night. Just maybe the police have other priorities – clearing the town centre, securing the police station. Who would have the tenacity for a stop and search in the middle of a brewing hurricane?

Glancing in the mirror, she sees the terror in her eyes and the pale-faced demeanour of a culprit.

You're not a killer, she tells herself. You're not even a criminal.

You've been fooling yourself. Can't even navigate a poison purchase without getting caught. And your planning skills? Speeding away from Nimbin's hinterland without heeding weather warnings? She can barely believe her naïvety. The poison. Get rid of the damn poison.

McCluskey can barely see beyond 20 metres or keep his eyes open with the rain coming at him in torrents. The crazy bitch with the poison? No sign of her. Yet. And the way McCluskey is breathing right now, his own demise may soon come to pass – the wind is nearly blowing him to the ground.

McCluskey lets out a heavy sigh that would rouse the dead if anyone could hear him. Fieldwork mate, he tells himself. This task force will all be over soon.

He hears an engine in the distance and raises his head. He shines the torch in the direction of the car and trudges forward through deep puddles.

She can barely see the distant figure in yellow nylon through the storm. Her heart is jumping up and down; her cheeks on fire. Jesus Christ, the officer is running towards the car now. She shoves the gear lever into park and glances once again at the passenger floor. The hip flask is lying loose on the mat, clearly visible if he looks in that direction. Talia stares straight ahead and, out the corner of her eye, sees him slowing to a standstill and yelling something. She's breathing rapidly and swallowing hard; all clarity of thought has escaped.

Come clean, damage limitation? The cop will never buy it.

All she can hear now is music on her car stereo. Techno and a beautiful female voice chanting 'Come back' every three seconds or so. Moby? The CD must have already reverted to track one, 'Honey'.

She lowers her right hand from the steering wheel and turns up the volume. Thuds of base and chants, southern black chanting and slide guitar, are interspersed beautifully with the mixing of the decks. Yes, yes, yes. Just stay here, in *that* world, she says to herself.

But the song also reminds her of Jeff, just after they began dating. How he had the confidence to get up in the middle of a dance floor, by himself, and jive. The whole bar faced him and he drank it all up without a smidgeon of self-consciousness. Girls smiled at him and salivated over his body. No other man had the balls to dance to this music, to mimic the chants, to allow for the interludes and change in styles from live to afro to techno. Talia had barely contained her excitement – her man being the envy of every woman in the place. Then he'd swivelled and pointed at her. She loved knowing that he was all hers.

A long time ago now.

Sit here and let the music play, that is all she can do now; to suspend the terror, to recall happier times, that awesome first summer together.

Perversely, she still misses him sometimes. Come back, she thinks of Jeff, bring back that part of you I loved: the excitement, the parties, the easy life. "Sometimes," she muttered, knowing it could never come back – not after the real Jeff kicked in: the narcissism, the boy who never grew up, the temper and the adultery.

Was it all an act, a sideshow to satisfy his need for attention?

She can't hear the policeman's voice anymore, just sees his squinted eyes beneath his hood. Seems to be yelling. He's coming around to the driver's side.

McCluskey thumps the driver's window and screams, "shut – your – engine". The wind is ferocious, but he can hear thuds of base on the stereo.

The woman lowers her window halfway, trying to shield her face from the diagonal rain smacking her.

McCluskey places a hand at his temple to block the rain slapping his own face. He sticks his head inside. The rain deflects off his raincoat onto the woman's lap. Still, that music is blaring, penetrating his skull. He yells at her to turn off the music.

She won't look at him, frozen on the seat. Something's not right.

He casts his eyes rapidly around the car. He can see her

handbag and… yes just beside it, a hip flask. He pauses. If he reaches in to turn down the stereo, his left elbow could extend into her face. The road underfoot is slippery. If he slips, his elbow could strike her. No bust would be worth that, all the complaints, the legal – not for a hipflask of poison.

What is that smell in here? Jesus Christ. The woman must have pissed in her knickers.

He slowly removes his head, pulls his neck in, and orders for her to wind up the window, which she does in an instant. He reaches for his walkie talkie, ponders his options as the rain batters him.

He could arrest the bitch for disobeying police orders? Yes, there's the hip flask; it justifies detaining her for a breath test and bust her for the poison. But, Jesus Christ, they wouldn't be too pleased back at the station – five hours of paperwork just for public insolence. He wouldn't be home until six, and Rebecca and Sofia would be scared to death in this. He bites his lip and lets the ensuing court proceedings play out in his head.

Me: "I saw a hipflask."

Defence Counsel: "Really? You stuck your head into the defendant's car. Was there any indicia of intoxication or drug usage?"

Me: "No."

Defence Counsel: "No? Then your search was clearly unlawful, you had no authority to be inside her vehicle."

McCluskey lets out a sigh and looks back into the car. Jesus Christ. All seems quite messy. He points his arm out, directing her to drive on.

Wagga Wagga: Two Years Later

McCluskey sits on the sofa. Three o'clock now and his police career is stagnant. Nobody is making any bold career appointments anytime soon. The Fitzgibbon Inquiry is in the fact-building stage and the public have been invited to inform their office of any information disclosing police misconduct. Reports of bribes, drug dealing, cash for comments and everything right down to the uniform laundry contracts have been exposed.

He switches on the television looking for sports news. He's heard about the big European soccer game happening at the weekend. Two rival Turkish clubs have reached the knockout stages of the Champion of Champions for the first time ever. The games are to be played in Berlin and German police are worried about an upsurge in looting and violence. The toxic combination of Galatasaray and Fenerbahce fans has the police chief on alert. The news is broadcasting his press conference about hooligans apprehended in a city hotel with knives and knuckle dusters.

McCluskey raises his eyes and shakes his head. He's never understood the perverse pull of sports fanaticism. He compresses his lips wistfully and changes channels. The US presidential candidate Barrack Obama is on stage with some musician called Moby. Obama's dancing and jigging and twisting his hips in between out-of-place fist pumps. Dressed in shorts and a t-shirt, he's doing an ambitious act of pretending he's on familiar terrain, as if to say, 'This ain't no big thing'. It looks pathetic to McCluskey.

Moby, on the other hand, is crouched forward with a slide guitar and his fingers run open down the fret board. As natural as can be.

Suddenly McCluskey's heart jumps, eyes widen – the music, it's that damn song again. That unforgettable concoction of jive, southern African chants interspersed with clapping and chanting of 'Honey come back'.

He stands up and walks around the living room. He can still see that woman's stunned gaze and hear her damn music blaring from the car stereo. She was in the papers a few days after he pulled her over – arrested for murder.

Still on trial, somehow the crazy bitch still isn't locked away.

He thinks of the lyrics, now etched in his head, 'honey come back'. Honey. How long had it been since he'd heard that word? His wife Beck is bored with him. They're just hanging on. Could he ever get their love to come back?

He scratches the side of his head. He wouldn't know where to start.

He bites his lip and stands, lets out a sigh. Thinking about that woman has him thinking about that old farmer prick, Douglas James – still unhappy with the size of his fine for touching up his worker. He's been spouting up north about it, probably looking for a trade off, some retribution.

Maybe it was time, McCluskey thought, to pay him another visit?

About 'Honey Coming Back'

I love reading crime novels and wanted to craft a story written from multiple perspectives. I am intrigued by different people's motives and characteristics, exploring why people do certain things in life – their choices and perceptions fascinate me. Music can also help explore people's motivations and so I used my inspiration track, 'Honey' by Moby, as a way of both connecting and exploring my characters' choices. The lyrics of the track have an ambiguous meaning; yet, on hearing them, the track conjures very different memories for both Talia and McCluskey – as it may for readers also.

Author: Peter Fagan

Peter Fagan lives in Mosman and he has a strong interest in fictional crime writing.

True Believers

Phil Burgin

24 February 1920. Munich, Germany

As soon as Karl mentioned politics, Martin had threatened to split.

"I thought we were going for a few quiet beers," growled Martin. "Noisy ones are also fine, but I'm not spending my last few Marks listening to shitty speeches from egghead scholars who've never served, but think they know what's best for the country."

Karl glanced at the wad of notes in his hand. "Alright, I'll buy the beers. Does that help?"

"Sure, but I still won't be listening." said Martin.

Karl gave his head a rueful shake. "It's important to show these bigots we won't stand by while they keep spewing out their hateful messages."

Martin shrugged. "Sorry, didn't hear anything after 'you're buying'."

Karl shot him a hard look before picking up his pace. "Come on, I don't want to be late."

Karl and Martin gripped their long coats tightly around them to ward off the icy wind sweeping through the old town square. Underfoot, damp slippery cobbles shimmered in the pale light cast from street lamps. The men bumped their way through the crowded square, filled with people hurrying home from work. Their destination, the Hofbrauhaus Beer Hall, a sprawling, neo gothic building, was at the far end of the square. Dim yellow light glowed in the many windows of the four-storied inn. Karl recognised a man loitering beneath the street lamp outside the beer hall. He waved and the man responded in kind.

"Dieter, how are you my friend?" said Karl.

"I'm well," he replied. "But I'd much rather be inside with a beer than out here freezing my balls off."

Karl laughed. "So why wait out here?"

"Hoping reinforcements might arrive." Dieter smiled "And I see you've brought some with you."

"Yes," said Karl. "This is Martin. However, he has no interest in politics."

Dieter looked Martin up and down. "I'm Dieter. Pleased to meet you." He offered his hand. "Welcome brother, we need all the help we can get fighting these bastards."

"Calm yourself, Dieter," said Karl. "We're here to stand against them using our voices not our fists." He threw an arm around Dieter's shoulder. "You know which room they're in?"

"Upstairs in the Festival room," said Dieter. "The meeting may have kicked off already."

"Then let's go."

Karl hurried inside and bounded up the stairs to the Festival room, the others a few steps behind. The room was lined with long tables occupied by men, old and young, many with their hands wrapped around a beer stein. Large wooden chandeliers hung low over the tables in contrast to the cavernous arched ceilings plastered in neo classical art. Dieter took one look around the crowded room, turned to the others and smiled.

"I'm off to find the bar." Dieter slipped into the crowd like a ghost.

"Are all of your friends like him?" asked Martin.

"Who? Dieter?" said Karl. "No, he's just young. He thinks the best way to solve problems is with a big club."

"And what problems are you trying to solve?"

Karl gave him a hesitant smile. "You'll see soon enough."

Despite the crowd, the room wasn't filled with the rowdy noise associated with a large gathering at the inn. Karl heard snatches of quiet conversations from different corners of the room, however the majority of the crowd appeared to be focused on a speaker at the far end of the room. The man, even on a raised dais, was difficult for Karl to hear. He edged closer, casually leaning against the wall, trying to catch the speaker's words. He startled when Martin jabbed him in the ribs.

"Beer," Martin said, pointing toward the bar.

Karl rolled his eyes and weaved his way through the crowd, eavesdropping on the conversations around him as he waited to be served. Most were banal exchanges about family, jobs or the lack of, but nothing overtly political. Karl grabbed the beers and walked back over to Martin.

"Is this as exciting as it gets?" asked Martin, taking a sip as he pointed to the speaker.

Karl laughed. "Doctor Dingfelder not interesting enough for you?"

"The most boring nonsense I've heard for some time. Just banging on about how our low moral standards are why Germany is in the shit. The funny thing is, I thought it was because we lost the war. If I have to listen to much more of this, I'll need more beer."

"Careful," said Karl softly. "This room is full of angry folk who think they've been betrayed by the government. There's no money, no jobs, this country feels like it's on its knees. These people want a path back to glory and if it's sold to them on the back of racist propaganda, so be it."

Martin took a long sip on his beer.

Karl discreetly pointed to the corners of the room. "See those men standing in the corners? We call them the disciples."

In each corner of the room, a small group of three or four men were gathered. None held a drink in hand and they appeared to pay little attention to the speaker, seemingly just observing the room.

"They think their presence alone is enough to dampen any dissent," said Karl. "But they're also happy to throw their weight around if needed. They only want true believers in here."

Muted clapping travelled throughout the room, signalling the end of Dingfelder's speech. A few halfhearted cries of 'Deutschland' rang out, but they quickly faded out.

Karl watched Martin look from one corner to the next, unable to read his expression. He sipped on his beer and waited for Martin's blunt assessment. Dieter returned in the interim.

"There's a few more of us scattered around the room," said Dieter. "I didn't want to be too obvious. Felt like I was being watched."

"Try to blend in," said Karl. "But make sure you're with someone."

Dieter nodded and slipped back into the crowd.

"If you're planning a takeover, there aren't enough of you," said Martin.

"No, we're here to try and contain the spread of their racist ideas." Karl leaned in, speaking in a hushed whisper. "Hopefully things don't turn ugly."

Martin stared at him, eyes narrowed. "Guess I'd better drink up then." Martin drained his beer and held up the empty glass for Karl.

Karl had just returned with two more beers when the noise in the hall seemed to swell around him. A man, considerably younger than the previous speaker, had stepped onto the stage. He wore a dark suit in contrast against his pale skin. His hair, reflecting the dull yellow light from overhead, was plastered to his skull and incorporated a side part of military precision. His top lip brandished a small moustache that, at a distance, could almost be mistaken for a rash. He peered over the crowd with an assumed arrogance, as all eyes turned to him and the chatter subsided.

"Who's this guy?" asked Martin. Several heads turned and gave the pair disapproving looks.

"Hitler," whispered Karl. "Adolf Hitler… and he's dangerous."

The contrast in style with Dingfelder was stark. Hitler's words, delivered in short, passionate sentences, took aim at the incompetent leaders that signed the treaty that doomed their homeland to decades of suffering. Karl watched in awe at the immediate crowd response. Each sentence was met with approval, and with each cheer Hitler's tone became harsher, darker, turning to themes of racial vilification. Fists pumped the air in support of the verbal assault.

A man, seated at one of the long tables on the other side of the room, sprang to his feet, voicing his disapproval. Karl, agreeing with every word, instinctively applauded and scanned the room for more support. The man's immediate neighbours, however, attempted to silence him with boos and hisses; and when that failed, they pulled at his clothing, attempting to drag him back to his seat.

Two disciples moved swiftly towards the disturbance, grabbing hold of the man and dragging him out.

Karl nudged Martin. "We need to help him."

Martin, his eyes fixed on Hitler, barely acknowledged his friend.

Karl shook his arm. "Martin, I said: we need to help."

Martin shook his head as though clearing his thoughts. "What?"

"Come on," said Karl.

Karl weaved between the tables with Martin in tow. Around

them, opposing voices spread like spot fires only to be met with open hostility, and Karl feared the room could ignite at any moment. Hitler ploughed on undeterred.

"There." Karl pointed at the two disciples dragging the protester towards the closest exit.

"Stop!" shouted Karl. "Release him."

One of the disciples briefly turned and smiled, before forging ahead with their eviction.

The man continued yelling with all the volume he could muster, "Free speech! Free speech!"

But aside from a few turned heads, reactions were muted.

Martin pushed past Karl and grabbed the arm of one the men, who instantly turned, threw and connected with a closed fist against Martin's temple.

Martin, momentarily stunned, responded before he was set upon by two more disciples, appearing from nowhere.

As Karl rushed in to help, members of the crowd got to their feet, their faces red and angry, screaming in his ears. Karl attempted to pull the men off Martin, but was pulled away by the mob.

He threw his arms around his head as kicks and punches rained on all exposed parts of his body. Stay on your feet. The thought circled through his mind as the attack continued, until the floor dropped away and he was flying over a set of stairs.

The impact was heavy and with three more bounces he was lying on the polished wood at the bottom of the stairwell.

Another body lay across his chest. Karl wriggled out from underneath and sat up. His heart was thumping, but relief flooded over him as he realised the crowd hadn't chased them down the stairs. He pushed himself to his feet, wincing as different parts of his body protested. Blood dripped from the end of his nose and he recoiled in pain as he touched a large gash on his forehead. Still dazed, Karl stared at the other two sprawled on the landing. One of them, Martin, groaned and rolled over. Karl offered his hand but Martin waved it away and stood up, bending his neck from side to side.

"Quite a night out, you should invite me to more of these things." Martin laughed.

"Why are you laughing?" Karl snapped. "We could have been seriously hurt." He crouched to check on the other man. He recognised him from a party meeting. "Levi?"

The man nodded and pushed himself into a seated position against the wall.

"Are you okay?'

"Think so," Levi said. "You see? This is what happens to anyone who challenges them."

"So why challenge them then?" Martin said bluntly.

Levi glared him. "Did you hear what that lunatic was saying? Do you not see your friend's face?" Levi pointed up the stairs, his arm stiff with anger. "He's blaming Jews for everything that's wrong with our country and turning those people against us… against their own countrymen."

"You're Jewish?"

"I'm German…and yes, I'm also Jewish."

"But they're just fanatics," said Martin. "People aren't going to listen to that nonsense. Just ignore them and they'll go away. In a few months you won't even remember his name."

"I wish you were right, but you felt it yourself," said Karl. "I saw your face. You were sucked in just like the others. Tonight, they had two thousand. In a few months, it could be ten thousand. Those words he uses are like a disease, and it infects just by listening to them. If we don't contain it now it could lead us back into another war."

Martin laughed. "Let's be serious. No one could be that stupid. We just lost everything in the last one."

"That's the problem," said Karl. "The people up in that room feel they have nothing left to lose… and someone is offering to take it back. What would you do?"

13 May 2016. Munich, Germany

Alex and Kurt stood in Old Town square and stared at the police line outside the Hofbrauhaus. The damp cobblestones, wet from an earlier shower, glistened in light thrown up from the surrounding buildings. A group of four men stopped at the line of police and, after presenting identification, passed through the cordon and into the beer hall.

"Is it just luck that you pick the only beer hall in town that has a police barricade?" asked Alex.

"I wanted to show you some Munich culture while you're

here," said Kurt. "I didn't know it would be surrounded by police when I suggested it."

"Was there a riot or something? A murder perhaps? Or just too many drunken British tourists?"

"Not sure," said Kurt with a laugh. "I'll check."

Kurt walked towards the line of police, spoke briefly with an officer before returning to Alex.

"Apparently it's an AfD party meeting."

"Those right-wing nutters?" Alex looked shocked. "How could they be allowed to have a meeting in the same place Hitler started off? That was, like, one hundred years ago; and now this lot are in there preaching the same stuff?"

"That's democracy my friend. Apparently they went to court to get approval."

"So now our taxes are paying for their protection?" Alex shook his head. "It's like a red rag to a bull."

"I think that's the point. They want the attention. You can tell there's an election coming."

Alex turned to Kurt. "Let's try somewhere else then."

"Sure, there's another place just around the corner, though it doesn't have quite the same charm."

"But it has beer, right?

Kurt nodded.

"Then let's go." Alex glanced once more at the Hofbrauhaus. "Do you think anyone listens to that stuff anymore?"

Kurt shook his head. "Neo Nazis and a few of their friends maybe. In a couple of years we won't even remember AfD. Just ignore them, don't give them any air, and they'll eventually die out. Now, onto more important matters, Bayern are playing Dortmund at home this weekend and I happen to have a spare ticket if you're interested..."

24 September 2017

In the 2017 German elections, the AfD – Alternative for Germany – a party previously unrepresented in the Bundestag, became the third largest party with 12.6% of the vote. This is more than double the 5% threshold required to qualify for full parliamentary status.

About 'True Believers'

This story was inspired by the song 'Thought Contagion' by Muse. The song itself refers to being influenced by the beliefs of others, hence the idea of a contagion, as though those beliefs, false or otherwise, can be contracted like a disease. In the period referenced in the story, the precursor to the rise of the Nazi party, the views of Hitler and his party were not discredited. Instead they gained wider acceptance the longer they went unchallenged, despite their atrocious nature, and a hundred years on those beliefs are still tightly held by an increasingly confident portion of German society.

Author: Phil Burgin

Phil Burgin lives on the Northern beaches of Sydney, having been convinced to move there by his wife. He writes stories that emphasise the need to be connected to our environment. His previously published works include 'Bullets & Butterflies' as part of a previous Northern Beaches Writer' Group anthology, and 'The Caretaker' as part of the Northern Beaches Council 'Art & Words' project, *Portrait*. He lives with his wife, two children and two dogs. He is envious that both his children are much smarter than he, but keeps this a well-guarded secret. His lucky number is two. Or thirteen. He can't decide.

King, King Calowe

Millicent Davis

Alison is told to wear closed-in shoes by her father. "The sun's giving the asphalt a beating!" he says, looking up owlishly from the computer. He's spent the morning filling his computer keypads with plaster dust as he taps away in the slowest and most tedious way possible.

Her mother wanders back and forth, making frantic phone calls and watching over the two of them like an overseer.

Alison finds the comment about the weather a little odd because she isn't exactly an outdoor kind of person. Implicit in the statement is a warning, one she only notices when her mother looks up, cheeks flushed red from an argument held over the phone.

"There's one shop in Kellyville. They didn't pick up the phone, so we need you to drive out and check they have some in stock," she says. And there's a bit of a lie in that statement. We. As though someone other than her mother is inclined to care about beetles.

Alison shrugs the entire thing off. "Mum, not to be a bother, but Kellyville is, like, three hours away."

"Well, I don't see you doing anything else useful!" her mother replies with a raised eyebrow and an expression that suggests they're on the verge of a massive argument.

Alison shrugs again. "Whatever." Then she wanders outside and is hit in the face with a blast of heat. Her father is clearly wrong – the sun isn't beating down on the asphalt below, it is performing a brutal act of unprovoked battery assault! The police should be called, the sun carted off to prison; where all his golfing buddies would inevitably defend him as a perfectly nice fellow. That's just the way these types of things go.

Alison decides to phone a friend, because she isn't driving to Kellyville alone; then she spends the entire drive moping.

Matt, the friend, doesn't bother to asks questions, he just smiles and says, "It's always nice to go for a drive", which is one of the reasons he's one of Alison's favourite people.

When they get there, the parking lot is full. Who'd want to go out on a day like today? Alison thinks to herself.

They park what feels like a kilometre down the road and are forced into the horrible melting heat that lurks like some kind of crushing predator outside the car.

"It's quite hot out," Matt says and it's all Alison can do not to glare at him.

It's just the kind of awkward conversation starter that doesn't leave any place to go. She can't disagree with him; it is hot outside. She can't say something like 'did you know Australia has an ozone hole' because then she risks him replying that he is aware of the ozone hole, which would be embarrassing.

She shrugs. "We've had hotter."

"Have we?" Matt says.

Which is also awkward; at least she supposes it is, after all there aren't too many words for an interaction that leave you feeling uncomfortable. So, they stand there in the street for a moment; wedged between the red brick houses and the endless dying gardens, neither saying anything.

Matt takes a long sip of a juice he's brought with him and pulls a face. He makes a show of looking at the container, turning it around. He raises an eyebrow and pulls off a look of utter scepticism that only he can manage.

"So, Kellyville and Christmas beetles?" he asks, walking another few metres.

She follows, feeling a little attacked by the question. Obviously, he isn't trying to be critical. Well, he might be… he could be trying to make a passive jab or some kind of underhand remark, but she is fairly sure that he is simply asking a question. That's the problem with asking a question, you run the risk of criticising the person you're asking. Have they given you too little information? Do you suspect they don't know the answer? Is it something they won't want to answer? The worst part, she supposes, is that you can never really know if it's one of the above before you've asked it. So, she simply says, "My grandmother wants them for Christmas."

She makes a point of not mentioning that her grandmother is dead, because it isn't important; and she makes a point not to glare at him, because – and she has to remind herself of this – they are good friends. He isn't trying to be cruel or condescending. It isn't a purposeful jab, she hopes.

"Why?" Matt says.

She stares at Matt; Matt stares back at her. He is waiting for an answer and a small part of Alison's brain has to run over the entire conversation to find out what he is asking. As she realises what the question is, she thinks that she should probably explain why she has driven him to Kellyville on a day when it is, like, 45 degrees; while he is still nice and neat, before he melts away.

Honestly, the fact that Matt let himself get driven here without asking the specifics is pretty incredible. But now the pause has gone on too long. He is staring at her unblinkingly as though to ask, 'Why have you taken me to a distant and isolated location? Why are you being so weird?'

She doesn't really have an answer, so she simply says. "My Nan says you can't have a good Christmas without Christmas beetles." Then she smiles, and he awkwardly smiles back. Mentally she corrects her statement to 'my Nan said', and it feels like a lie, but it would take too much time to say so.

"Ah, well I never really understood Christmas beetles, they're a bit odd really." He glances at her and it's all she can do not to yell at him, despite the fact that they are really good friends and she's just being an idiot about things.

They keep walking.

Eventually they catch a glimpse of the store. It's big and white with a frankly disgusting façade. It declares itself as a 'mini-pet-shop', which Alison finds strange because the shop itself is quite large. She shares this theory with Matt, who replies, "Perhaps it's the pets that are mini."

Then she feels like a complete idiot, because obviously that's what the sign means, and now she's worried that Matt thinks she is lying about not getting it, in an attempt to be cute. Of course, it is mini-pet shop. Maybe she is an idiot?

Then she's just standing there, frozen like an utter fool, and Matt asks if she's okay and she has to reply and say something stupid like, "yeah, I'm just really hot". Then she has to worry about him interpreting it as double-entendre.

The moment they step into the building, with its ample air conditioning and red and white checker pattern tiles, she feels a bit better. The building smells like bugs and is quite large, even if the clutter of cages and insect noises give it a claustrophobic feeling.

Matt wanders ahead, quick to look about the endless terrariums. He goes into the stacks to look at a terrarium that Alison thinks contains a bright red snail.

Now that he has gone off on his own, she begins to rethink everything she has said to Matt over the last few hours. Maybe he's mad at her? Or maybe he just likes snails?

She ignores the worry gnawing at her stomach and approaches the woman at the counter. "So, I'm looking for some Christmas beetles?" Alison hears herself say.

The woman looks up at her and blinks. Then with a weary shrug of her shoulders, she makes an inexplicable gesture. "We don't keep seasonal beetles."

Alison stares back at her.

The woman has auburn hair pulled back into a bun.

"Oh," Alison says.

The woman returns to watching something on an iPad propped up against an empty terrarium at the counter.

———◯———

The car ride home is cool, pleasant even. Alison keeps looking over at Matt and feeling guilty. He hasn't said anything smug or condescending, even though she feels he probably should. Maybe he could say something like 'Well this was pointless' or perhaps 'Why'd you drag me all the way out here then?', then it would be over. But instead, he is halfway through an admittedly funny story about his sister and her friends, and Alison isn't quite sure what to do.

"Sorry for bringing you out here," she says, regretting the words immediately. To defend herself she bows her head and makes a show of focusing on the road.

Matt shrugs, apparently unconcerned about the sudden excursion he's been brought on, about his sweat-drenched clothing and the fact that she's dragged him into a room with several hundred spiders, which – now she thinks about it – he may be deadly afraid of. That's just something else to worry about. It's not like she can ask him at this point 'hey are you afraid of spiders? Or is that Liam?'

Matt doesn't respond to the apology. He simply says, "I always enjoy a good walk. The temperature's not great for it, but it is a nice time." It isn't quite an answer. He is very polite about it, but it makes her heart pound because it is so evasive.

Alison isn't quite sure if she is going to have a panic attack.

Then Matt says, "You know, you can probably just go and find a Christmas beetle. I mean, it's nearly Christmas… they'd be around."

"Really?" Alison says, noting how dismissive it sounds.

"People, like, catch them; they have entomology groups and stuff." Matt searches on his phone.

"Someone found a bunch in Dural," he continues.

She nods politely. But she isn't going to Dural, not for Christmas beetles, not even for a cash prize with diamonds. "Don't worry about it, it doesn't matter all that much," she says, and now he is frowning.

"But your grandmother wanted them," He looks a little worried; he rubs his neck and pushes hair back behind his ears. Only Matt would worry about failing someone else's grandparents.

"My grandmother is dead," Alison replies with a shrug.

Matt raises an eyebrow at that, but he doesn't seem surprised. "Oh, I'm sorry…"

"Yeah it's like, well, you know when you are young and you have Christmas parties at your grandparents house?" She doesn't leave him time to respond, it isn't a real question after all. "We'd stay over at out Nan's and she had this big old house. It had a balcony, and the Christmas beetles would get stuck on the flyscreen doors, so the morning before we opened presents or anything we'd collect all the Christmas beetles, then the next day we'd let them go."

"Oh", Matt replies. "That's… nice."

"Up your wings and fly away, so the rhyme goes. I think my mum wants something like that again, so she's been harassing people trying to get Christmas beetles."

"People used to worship ladybugs for the same reason. Because they're seasonal, people attach sentimental memories to them."

"Right," Alison replies feeling a touch annoyed. She doesn't need an explanation.

They sit in silence for a little while.

The landscape starts to go dark, and the world almost fades away, and it reminds her of a memory. A small niggling part at the back of Alison's mind thinks: wouldn't it be nice to have Christmas beetles again? Like when she'd sit on her grandmother's lap and watch the sun go down and the sky turn a murky black, and the golden beetles would get stick in the flyscreen – back when they could take Christmas beetles for granted and pick them up to show to her parents.

They continue driving in almost silence.

Alison can't help but feel a touch of melancholy.

Matt jiggles his leg. "So, last week," he starts talking, "I ran into this guy I know; I sometimes see him when I'm at the local grocery store. And there he is wandering up and down the beach… completely nude! It was pretty scandalous."

"Why?"

Matt gives her a look that suggests it's a peculiar question. Maybe she has no ability to tell peculiar questions from normal ones?

Matt opens his mouth, then frowns. "That's a good question actually. I didn't think to ask him that."

"Oh. What did you say to him?" She glances across at Matt, not quite paying attention to the conversation.

"I told him it wasn't a nude beach and he left," Matt says, apparently contemplative. "Although, now I consider it, this story would probably have been a lot more fun if I had asked him why."

"Well, there's always next time," Alison replies, then kicks herself. It is hardly likely that Matt is regularly going to find nude men at the beach.

Outside the car, it's all shadows and trees now, which tower over the road. It's the kind of place where people dump bodies. It's creepy and menacing. The gum trees cut an uncomfortable silhouette against the pastel pink sky and Alison finds herself staring out at them while trying to find a witty reply to Matt's story about the nude man.

Then, in the dark, she sees a flash of gold and she swears that if it's a Christmas beetle and she drives on she'll regret it. As silly as the whole thing is, it's beginning to make her think of her grandmother, of the red silk shawls she wore and the sound of ABC Sunrise she watched religiously, and of course the peppery scent of cornflowers. So, she pulls the car over and Matt doesn't say anything; he simply gets out of the car with her.

"I thought I saw one," she says.

Matt nods and scuffs at the ground with his rather nice shoes. Leaves and branches are kicked up and he eyes the trees with his hands in his pockets and a distant look on his face.

She feels a little silly bringing him out here, because now she's nearly certain he is the one afraid of spiders, because before taking each step forward he waves a hand in front of himself to check for spiderwebs.

The golden glint of a beetle's wings doesn't reappear.

So they shuffle back to the car with its escape from the still stifling twilight heat.

Matt's clothes are a mess; her clothes are a mess. Although her clothes don't matter as much as Matt's. This trip was her suggestion; he was just along for the ride.

There is an obvious solution though: after she gets home, she'll never speak to Matt again. She could cut off all contact. She'd change schools. She'd even move to another country.

It is all too embarrassing.

Matt glances at his phone again and gives her a smile. "So do you think there's any chance we'll run into another naked bloke if we go down the beach next week?"

Her strategy of avoidance is paying off. She's managed to put off going to the beach. She's also shaken off an invitation to go over to Matt's house to watch telly together. Although… she is quickly becoming bored with the complete lack of entertainment. Embarrassing herself in front of Matt might be mortifying, but it does pass the time effectively. So instead of doing anything fun, like looking for Christmas beetles to make her mother happy, she sits inside and carefully constructs a web of lies around why she can't hang out with Matt anymore.

Which – when she thought about it – is a weird thing to do. Maybe she is just an exceptionally strange person? Well, if she is, it isn't Matt's problem anymore. So, she lies on her couch feeling guilty about not being able to find Christmas beetles. Her family Christmas is now Christmas beetle-themed to keep her mother happy. While this is quite fun, it is also extremely grating.

Thump, thump, thump comes a knock on the door.

Alison manages to slide herself off the lounge.

Thump, thump, t-

She opens the door.

Matt gives her a friendly smile.

For a moment she panics. She's told him she's up the Central Coast with her parents, which – now she thinks about it – is a very silly lie. Now he'll know everything she's said is a lie.

But then she looks at Matt, and Matt doesn't seem at all that concerned by her presence. So, she goes to say something.

Matt waves her down like one would a panicked horse. "Look, everyone on Earth has some," he gestures, "event, ceremony, something that has significance to them, and that's hard. I just want to say, I let you take me to Kellyville," he pauses and grins, "and no amount of emotional suffering is equal to the hell that is Kellyville. There were spiders there! Spiders! To that end, I simply want to say that you are a monster Alison, and I won't forgive you." He's joking; he has to be.

She laughs. In fairness, it is very funny, and she is about to say so when he begins a harsh search of his coat.

He empties pockets, interior and exterior, and eventually finds a box. It's wrapped in the cheap chemist store wrapping paper that appears during the holiday season, with candy cane wielding reindeers and anthropomorphised baubles decorated with palm trees on a red and gold background.

"This is a shadowbox with a Christmas beetle in it. It kinda defeats the purpose of the whole thing. I mean the reason people are attached to Christmas beetles is that they come at a very particular time of year. They are temporal, seasonal. It's why you can't buy live Christmas beetles." He gives her a look that suggests he is about to be cheeky again. "You probably should have just bought one of these in the first place." Then he pauses and stares at her for a moment. "Onto other business, you have been very weird, and I would like you to stop it." He looks thoughtful.

She laughs again, not knowing what else to do.

"I'm being quite serious." He rattles the box. "This logically inconsistent Christmas beetle is dependent on you behaving more normally; not too normally of course, we couldn't have that, but more Alison-y."

Alison smiles, and wonders if there isn't another reason for Matt's visit. Something she would have to contemplate over the next few hours. She stands aside and beckons him into the house. "Alright, for a Christmas beetle, I guess you are owed that."

About 'King, King Calowe'

This story is based on a rhyme called King, King Calowe. Now a person might point to the differentiation between rhymes and songs, however there is a school of rhyme historians who theorise that the few remaining lines of King, King Calowe were a part of a larger oral chant. The thought is that, at some point, this mostly innocuous children's rhyme about ladybeetles was actually a ritual song or hymn. The translation into English likely saw the shortening of the song in order to maintain the rhyming scheme. I like this rhyme. I find its lyrics interesting, along with the near universal regard of ladybeetles as mystical creatures – from the Romans to the Germanics to parts of Scandinavia, this little red beetle is considered magical. In Australia of course we have our own little gold beetle, so I figured I would write a story about hunting for them. 'King King Calowe, Up your wings and fly away. Over land and over sea, tell me where my love might be.'

Author: Millicent Davis

Millicent Davis is a young aspiring environmental scientist who lives on Sydney's Northern Beaches and enjoys writing.

The Need For Witchcraft

Guy Hallowes

Scotland, 11th century

Double, double, toil and trouble;
Fire burn, and cauldron bubble,
Fillet of fenny snake
In the cauldron boil and bake;
Eye of newt and toe of frog,
Wool of bat and tongue of dog,
Adder's fork and blind worms sting,
Lizard's leg and owlet's wing,
For a charm of powerful trouble,
Like a hell-broth, boil and bubble.

Kenyan Highlands, early 1950s

My father, Rupert, owned and ran a productive mixed farm in the early 1950s, which included a large flock of about six hundred sheep. With the help of a well-trained dog, he used to count the sheep daily by running the flock up against a fence line. He noticed over a period of a few weeks that, every now and then, one or two would go missing. He always recounted and was almost never wrong.

Someone was stealing his sheep.

He had a discussion with my mother. "The police will just disrupt the whole place. They are most unlikely to find anything. The African constables are all Wakamba and the people here mostly Kikuyu…"

"What other options do you have?" Mum responded.

"Witchdoctor, there is a Kikuyu *Mganga* on a nearby farm. I'll go there."

"I don't believe in witchdoctors…"

"No, but our people do."

There had been a lull in the advent of missing sheep, but then it all started up again; first there were two sheep missing, then three the next night.

Having thought about the situation, and being sensitive to African culture, he decided to engage the local *Mganga* or witchdoctor.

Midweek, he asked all the male heads of the thirty-five families who worked on his farm to gather outside the barn he had just completed, which was a natural gathering place. They all met just after 3pm, when most knocked off work for the day; it was also convenient for his milkers, since the evening milking only started at 4pm.

Rupert had already fetched the *Mganga*, a short little man, who stood next to him dressed in an array of monkey and other animal skins. He also wore a monkey facemask and a collection of wooden gourds attached to his clothing that made distinct, deliberately disturbing, rattling sounds as he moved about.

Rupert explained to everyone in Swahili, "Someone or some people are stealing my sheep and the *Mganga* will tell us who is responsible."

The *Mganga* had built a small fire, in which he had placed the blade of a *panga* (a bush knife similar to a machete).

The men were aware of the theft since Rupert had mentioned it several times in recent weeks. The *Mganga* lined up the men and paraded up and down in front of them, staring at each man, rattling his gourds, trying to make the men nervous.

Rupert knew that the men understood and believed in the process; it was precisely what the local headman in their home villages would have done. They also believed that, if any of them were guilty, the *Mganga* would find them out.

The *panga* blade was now red-hot. The *Mganga* asked all the men to stick their tongues out and, having removed the *panga* from the fire, he ran up the line of men and very lightly touched each man's tongue with the red-hot *panga*. Rupert understood that the psychology of this practice was that if a man was innocent his tongue would still be moist and the red hot *panga* would have no effect. A guilty man's mouth would be dry and the *panga* would slightly blister the man's tongue.

The *Mganga* then ran up and down the line and pointed to a man in the middle of the line, saying in Swahili, "This man stole your sheep."

Rupert was disappointed. The *Mganga* had pointed to Waithiru, one of his employees. He had had high hopes for Waithiru, who had been with him now for three years.

Waithiru fell to his knees and admitted that he had stolen the sheep.

Rupert then dismissed the men and asked Waithiru to stay behind, which he did.

As the men ambled off, Rupert heard his senior Kikuyu tractor driver address the other men in Swahili: "Lupiti (that was how they pronounced Rupert) understands our traditions, the *Mganga* has found the man who stole the sheep. This is much better than getting the police, who would have asked us many silly questions and found out nothing. This was the best way."

Rupert asked the *Mganga* to wait in his car and then said to Waithiru in his native Kikuyu, which Rupert spoke fluently, "Waithiru, I am disappointed in you. Why did you steal the sheep?"

Waithiru looked abashed and whispered, "My father has paid six cattle as part of the bride price for my second wife, but I must find five hundred shillings and also a sheep for the wedding feast."

"You should have come to me. I would have lent you the five hundred shillings and given you a sheep for the feast."

Waithiru just hung his head.

"This is what will happen now. I will not dismiss you, but you will get no wages for six months – which will be five hundred shillings – and you can find your own sheep for the feast. If you do anything like that again, you will be in big trouble. Do you understand?"

Waithiru nodded. "*Asante sana Bwana.*" He and Rupert both knew the loss of wages would be inconvenient but cause little real hardship. Every workers' family was given weekly rations sufficient to feed the family with *posho* (maize meal) and meat from a recently slaughtered bull calf when it was available, which was most weeks. There was also a quarter acre allocated to each family where they could grow maize and vegetables, either for their own consumption or to sell; and each family was allowed to graze five head of cattle on the farm as well.

A relieved Waithiru slowly walked away.

"You were very generous," Mum said afterwards.

"He made a mistake, he now knows that. He has a wife and three children. What would they have done back in the Kikuyu Reserve? It's just an overcrowded dustbowl now. All I did was put him in the position he would have found himself in if he'd come to me in the first place. He will also be in bad odour with the rest of the labour – none of them will want to be put through the witchdoctor business again."

And none of them ever needed to be.

About 'The Need for Witchcraft'

The famous 'Double, double, toil and trouble' lyrics chanted by the witches in Shakespeare's Macbeth (Act 4 Scene 1) has always reminded me of this true story about my father and the witchdoctor. Witchcraft has been part of humanity forever, before even religion. Perhaps there's good reason why.

Author: Guy Hallowes

Guy Hallowes has lived in many different countries: born in Kenya, and qualified as a chartered accountant in the UK, he has also lived in South Africa, Botswana, and Canada, before settling with wife Diana and their four children on Sydney's leafy North Shore. A senior executive in a major international publishing company for twenty years, Guy always harboured a wish to write – a wish that has now been more than fulfilled with six novels published and now a seventh one: 'Joe'. His website is: www. guyhallowes.com

Treachery

Elise Robertson

Alyssain was choked with people. Everything and everybody was so close together that it would not take much for pestilence or fire to rip through. Even the merchants were not immune in their stone houses. After the battle and subsequent siege of Alyssai Castle by the advancing Toryn army, those who survived were struck down with the fever. This is where so many died.

The king lounged on his throne, dressed in a doublet slashed with gold silk, lapis blue hose and leather heeled shoes.

His favoured advisor glared at me coldly with shrewd dark eyes, her sharp chin canting upward. Her cruel smirking mouth whispered into his ear, no doubt advising him to dismiss us before we could even make our request.

Perhaps she wanted to fumigate our travelling clothes – my best woollen gown, cloak and leather slippers? My Northern cloak was excessively warm but I dared not remove it. Aaron, handsome in his best russet woollen tunic, thick leather breeches and polished fur-lined boots, stood at attention by my side.

"Landholders from the Far Northern Wards," announced the high steward. "What brings you here among us this morn?"

I bowed low. "Your majesty, King Darlos, we sent word to your court that the Far North is plagued by a terrible monster. Cattle have been slaughtered. Crops are flattened. Without help, our people cannot survive the approaching winter. Sire, we beg that you send soldiers to slay this monster. We are in need of a protector to safeguard our lands. We would be in your debt." I bowed again.

Courtiers muttered around us. Brilliant gemstones glittered in the women's hair, at their throats and wrists, so beautifully they looked like fallen stars as they stood beside their husbands.

"Has anyone seen this… monster?" a knight enquired, standing amongst the crowd.

Those courtiers closest to the king's dais laughed, their ladies tittering behind their fans.

I noted the knight's delicate silk doublet; while beads of sweat dripped down my back beneath my heavy garments. Two of the four huge stone hearth-fires were lit, although the crowded Lower Hall scarcely needed it. High glass windows flooded the hall with warm golden light.

"No, majesty. But I have seen cattle dead from frost or wolf attack. This is unlike anything we have ever seen."

"Perhaps it is a kitsune?" the knight called out to the king. "They are common enough in…"

"Kitsune bury their kills," I interrupted, my voice strong. "They prefer rotted meat. These animals are left freshly dead in the fields. Whatever hunts them is something unknown." I thought of my remaining goats huddled together, secure in a neighbour's barn. Already several of our herd had been picked off.

The king's fingers drummed against the arm of his throne. Finally, he spoke. "What proof do you have? Witnesses?"

Aaron bowed again, beckoning to Thom the butcher from our village to carry in and unwrap the evidence.

Deep slashes were cut into the cleaved calf's back and neck, suggesting huge claws and teeth had hacked into the animal. Its legs were shattered as though thrown or dropped from a terrible height. Mould furred the grizzly remains.

Courtiers shrieked. Some fainted. Others turned away, covering their mouths to avert the open retch of bile. A shocked silence followed.

The king stared at the carcass without emotion.

I appealled to him again. "Sire, in the last siege of Alyssain, cats, horses and rodents were this city's last resort for sustenance. Please, sire, do not allow this to also happen to people of the North."

The king smiled with apparent benevolence, straightened his luxurious velvet doublet, which matched his pale olive eyes. "And we have kept our city of Alyssain safe. But armed Alyssain soldiers and the king's knights are not necessary in this case – this peculiar violence will soon be halted by the Far North's deep winter." The king's face did not colour, nor did his features change. Yet his smile, his smooth voice and studied indifference certainly concealed his underlying disdain of our plight.

A small number of ashen ladies still wailed softly into their lace handkerchiefs.

"Thank you, majesty," Aaron said, bowing deeply again. His arm encircled my waist and ushered me away towards the petitioners' antechamber.

Another petitioner instantly stepped forward before the king, in our place.

We left the calf, with its gut-turning stench, resting in the centre of the flag-stoned room.

I stepped through the doorway. "I must speak with you, sire."

"I thought your petition had been dispensed with," pronounced the king, not bothering to look up from the table in his private antechamber.

Aaron remained in the stone passageway.

"Search her!" the king ordered, still not raising his head.

A guard roughly inspected my garments, found nothing.

"I have my tongue, majesty," I responded. "That is sharp enough."

The king halted his writing and glared at the parchment in front of him.

"Please, send us your soldiers to help fight this monster," I implored, my voice breaking.

Silence.

"I am much afraid to be here, pleading for help." My voice rose. "But I am also tired of the empty promises of kings."

"How dare you!" the king thundered, rising from his desk to face me at last.

"If you had committed your soldiers after the first alarm had been relayed," I accused, rushing now, "I would not be here, would I?"

The king glared at me, his restraint almost as frightening as his temper. His neck was flushed; his knuckles white, as if he sorely wished to wring my neck. Suddenly he directed a savage kick, sending his chair crashing to the floor.

I stood my ground. If the king was trying to frighten me, he had succeeded. But I couldn't let him detect my fear. "I would rather die here, now, by your hand, sire, than starve slowly, later, in the cold." My throat tightened. I was lowly born and a woman. Few would notice or care if he killed me. Someone could simply fling my body over the walls or bury it in one of his ornamental gardens.

He eyed me, as if surprised I wasn't cowering before him or bursting into tears; then he paced in front of his desk, thinking. "I have given my oath – before gods and men. What would people think if their king went back on his word?" he asked sharply.

"If you will not provide us with soldiers, I will have no choice but to rally a protector myself."

The king growled.

"Words can be slippery fish," I persisted. "Politicians and

diplomats are masters of saying 'yes' and 'no' at the same time. We need actual, real help."

Someone behind me cleared their throat, interrupting the argument.

"What is it now, Lord Harel?" the king snapped.

A knight entered the room, his mighty calloused hands clasped awkwardly in front of him. The king's guard hadn't confiscated *his* sword. "Sire, have you given more thought to my request?" his voice was familiar. This was the knight who had spoken up earlier in the Lower Hall.

The king exhaled.

"The Lady Ileana?" the knight prompted.

The king looked at me, his mouth twitching into a cruel smile, green eyes bright. "You wish to marry, Lord Harel? You are also a man of the North – so take these two Northerners, your men and any soldiers who volunteer, and destroy their monster. On your successful return, you will have my blessing, and Lady Ileana's family will be formally linked to yours by marriage."

"Your highness," Lord Harel bowed gratefully, then motioned for the guard to escort us from the room as he left.

Lord Harel and his men spent the next few weeks journeying with Aaron and I, tracking reports of devastation from frightened villagers and farmers as we travelled closer to our own region. Finally we dismounted in a clearing in the midst of a dense

Northern forest, and cautiously approached a wide stone tower, the monster's rumoured stronghold.

We crept up a flight of stone steps and entered a raised reception hall, airless and foul. The floor was sodden with shit. It was dark and the room hummed. Anyone or anything could be concealed within: watching, waiting.

There was a sickening crunch as one of our party moved forward. The soldier peered down at his foot. "A bone, sire," he reported grimly.

"Keep together," Lord Harel breathed. "We have found its lair."

A hushed sigh, and the rotten stench suddenly became more oppressive than before; then something heavy dug deep between my shoulders.

I screamed in pain without thinking. "Get away from me!"

The weight only dug in, leaning more heavily.

"Devil spawn!" Lord Harel yelled, drawing his sword, as did his men.

The beating of wings and screeching echoed throughout the tower. The terrible weight left my shoulders.

"Light," a compelling voice commanded in the gloom.

My pain-watered eyes adjusted to a sudden brightness.

A massive owl's eyes feasted upon me, eerily bright. A gust of wind from its tremendous flapping wings knocked soldiers to the ground. With a screech, it flew to a high rafter, alighting beside a roped animal carcass.

No, not a carcass. It was a body, or at least the remains of a human body. It swung slowly, the bright light revealing deep gouges where flesh had been stripped away. Mildew-yellow bones poked through and writhed with flies. The creak of the rope and the drone of flies made for an uncomfortable sound in the silence.

"Gods be with us!" Lord Harel spat. "Shield wall!"

Shoulder-to-shoulder we closed ranks. The heavy leather of my jerkin now had rents where the creature had torn it. It must have noting the dull gleam of the chainmail worn by Harel's men, and thought me the weakest. It would come to regret that choice.

"Archers!" Lord Harel commanded.

The most noble man Aaron and I had come to know, Harel was obeyed immediately.

The owl descended through the onslaught of arrows, landing in front of us pricked with a dozen of them. It did not weaken or wane, but instead shifted its form. Snow white feathers rippled into waist-length silver white hair. Pearl-white skin shimmered like moonlight on water.

The shimmering woman plucked out an arrow shaft struck deep in her shoulder and threw it clattering to the floor. She continued, arrow by arrow, without flinching. Then she strode towards us, feet bare, silvery gown flowing, golden girdle luminous. An overpowering floral fragrance preceded her, masking the cloying rottenness of death.

"Soft mortals," she sneered, every wound on her body flawlessly healing. "Did you really think it would be so easy to destroy me? Have you not heard of Khalida the Shapeshifter?" With inhuman speed, Khalida flew behind an archer and drew a talon across his throat like a razor.

He slumped lifeless to the floor, not even having time to cry out.

Without hesitating, Khalida slammed into another archer, digging her unnaturally sharp fingernails as predatory talons across his neck.

He staggered back in surprise, clutching at his throat, before crumpling to the floor.

Khalida took to the air again. "I am no monster. I am the one that stands between your pathetic little towns and ruin. Plagues of rats, wild dogs and kitsune – that is what your overpopulations face without me curbing your excesses. Nature takes care of its own. Predators exist for a reason. Mortals have become soft. They have forgotten what it takes to survive. But King Darlos understands." Khalida smirked and pointed up towards the swinging corpse. "Lord Harel, is this form familiar?"

We all looked.

Khalida directed another shaft of light toward the corpse.

Around the body swung a crumpled silk gown stiffened and dark with blood.

"Princess Biella of Toryn!" gasped Lord Harel. "The king's betrothed – his promised allegiance to Toryn, to end the siege. What have you done?"

"Not what I have done, what your king has agreed to do."

"You… you've destroyed the peace!" shouted the closest soldier, shocked.

"We are all certain to die!" another soldier groaned.

"Alyssain cannot survive another war with Toryn," Lord Harel roared, fierce tears in his eyes. "There are too few soldiers left!"

Khalida's smile glittered. "Ah, but there is a remedy for that. King Darlos and I have forged a secret weapon – a sword powerful enough to kill any enemy of the one who holds it."

"King Darlos," Aaron snarled, "would never throw in his lot with this demon!"

"Ah, but he has. And he commissioned me to create a potion for you, his brave soldiers." She gestured to a pewter cauldron simmering gently in a far corner. "Dragon's blood. The hands of a Redcap. Dried maidens' tears – thank you, Princess Biella!" she smirked again. "Place a mere drop into any corpse-soldier's mouth and it shall walk and fight again."

"Monstrous!"

"Madness!"

"Murderer!"

Lord Harel was silent. His face had turned fiery red, with eyes wide and nostrils flared, as though he had been backed into a corner. "Treachery," he muttered. "Our king has betrayed us!" Suddenly he lunged at Khalida. Each thrust and slash desperate, his breathing ragged. His hatred was cold and relentless. "You will die for controlling him with your treachery!"

The shapeshifter laughed coldly. "Trusting loyal mortal! A king does not have friends – only followers. Even then, every so often, a king will as likely put their head upon a spike as reward them for their loyalty. All people are weeds to be cut down before they rise too high. Did you really think you were special?"

Lord Harel wiped his forehead and stepped back. "Spears!" he shouted.

Those with spears hurled them at Khalida.

Shifting again to owl form, she wheeled about, dodging the missiles.

Harel ran at her as she changed form again.

His mighty arm swung his war hammer at Khalida's face, throwing his entire weight behind the blow.

It should have crushed bone when it hit her. Instead, with a crack, black spidery lines slithered across the silvery woman's jaw; then, glowing, disappeared. She grinned, then clawed at Harel's face with her talons.

He held off her next blow, backing away.

Aaron and the small troop of remaining men rallied around Harel for a final attack.

"This is doing piss all against her," Aaron panted, the cuts on his face raised. "We need to regroup."

"Wait," I hissed, glimpsing the hilt of a sword at the far end of the room. "Cover me," I called out to Harel.

Giving me a grim nod, Aaron, Harel and the remaining archers drew their bows, sending a torrent of missiles toward the shapeshifter.

Briefly distracted, Khalida's body bristled as arrows hit – at her side, back and throat.

I sprinted to the scabbard hanging on the wall, glancing back. Khalida's gaze flickered towards me.

In desperation Aaron flung his hunter's knife into her back.

It buried deep into Khalida's shoulder. She didn't bother to remove it; all attention was focused solely on me.

As I seized the sword and wrenched it from its feathered scabbard, a seething hiss forced her to glance momentarily back around.

Lord Harel and his men were at the simmering cauldron, levering it over with their spears.

A river of smoking filthy grey poison flooded across the stone floor.

"You disgusting wretches!" Khalida shrieked, as though they had just killed her own loathsome offspring.

I ran, sword in hand towards the other corner, trying to put some distance between Khalida and myself.

My boots skidded on slick shit. I hit the ground hard. A sharp shock of pain reverberated through my left leg, and skinned my forearms. "I'm fine, I'm fine, I'm fine," I told myself, angered and embarrassed.

With a piercing shriek, the shapeshifter turned and charged at me, talons raised above her head.

I rolled away as their piercing sharp tips ripped through my cloak.

Khalida arched again, ready to strike.

Without thinking, I lunged the sword forward into her stomach. Its blade sank deep, impaling her through and through. Slimy organs, fluid and blood sluiced out over my skin. Stomach roiling, I gritted my teeth and rammed the blade harder through her.

Blood from the fatal wound stained the creature's gown the colour of rotting flowers. It filled her mouth, staining her teeth a horrible pink.

"War is coming," she wheezed with her last breath, baring her teeth in triumph. "Ten thousand soldiers… will march… by spring. I have seen it." Then her body sagged.

I waited, still.

Her skin dulled, the whites of her eyes fixed, her lips paled blue. Only then did I pull the sword away, shoving her body away with my foot.

The sword blade glittered. Khalida's blood had seeped into the metal, turning it dark red.

Ringing filled my ears as I held it up – the clang and clamour of future battles beckoning and beguiling me, louder and louder. Blood-lust coursed through my veins and I had the sudden desire to use the sword to strike down those around me.

Unnerved, I quickly re-sheathed the sword in its scabbard.

The ringing abruptly stopped.

Lord Harel grabbed my arm. "We need to get the shapeshifter away from this unholy potion. Even the slightest drop could revive her corpse."

I limped alongside the others.

We pitched Khalida's inert body from the nearest window, down into the wilds below.

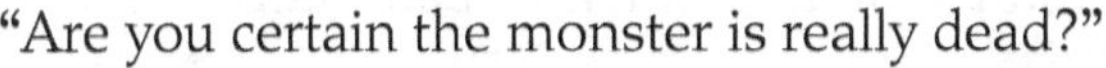

"Are you certain the monster is really dead?"

Courtiers crowded around the dais, where King Darlos leaned forward on his throne. He had a guarded look.

"Yes, your majesty."

The king laughed. "Well, Northerners, I suppose you want a reward?"

Liveried servants marched in hefting a number of sacks that spilled over with grain and others with vegetables.

It wasn't even half of what was needed.

Aaron's strong arm encircled my waist, the heat of his body warming me, *warning* me. This wasn't the time or place for objections.

"Thank you, your majesty. You have been most gracious." I bowed.

The king then beckoned Lady Ileana's family forward. "Lord Harel. In your absence, another suitor has unfortunately claimed Lady Ileana's hand, with my blessing. But I promised your families would be bound in marriage, so this is Lady Tara, her younger sister," the king drawled. "I am sure she will be just as suitable a bride."

Lord Harel's eyes were blank, his nose still clotted with blood.

Lady Ileana stood behind her sister with her head bowed.

Lady Tara was barely of age, her large grey eyes darting left and right, her thin body slightly trembling, as though expecting a pinch or slap at any moment. She was a pale plain imitation of her older sister.

"Sire." Harel bowed to the king, then to Lady Tara with stiff solemnity.

The king wrapped them all in a charming smile, called for wine and for the minstrels to recommence playing, then turned to his mistress to share a joke. Her own dark head bent within a breath of his majesty's ear, her delicate white hand shamelessly stroking a new black pearl necklace decorating her throat.

As though nothing had just happened.

As though King Darlos hadn't hoped to send Lord Harel and his men to their deaths.

As though his countless betrayals weren't personal for any of us.

I shivered, goosebumps prickling my arms. How hollow. How revolting. How… dangerous.

Lord Harel and Aaron sipped their proffered wine mechanically.

"The shapeshifter is dead, yet I fear the king is still the king," Harel admitted in a low voice. "He was never controlled. He only ever sends for one when one is needed; the rest of the time it is as if one doesn't exist. Like a toy or some amusement. There is more to ruling than this."

We moved to a quiet alcove where we could speak privately.

Lord Harel reached into his cloak lining and pulled out a medallion engraved with his family crest, along with a small heavy leather pouch. "I am returning to my estates in Averam –

there is much requiring my attention. Plans. Preparations. But you have my word, Northerners – the Far North Wards will have the protector they sought. I have sent men ahead, to keep watch until my return. They will spread word of what has happened here, and what happened… *there*. You still have your sword?" he asked me.

"I do."

"Then this is not the end, it is just the beginning. Where a king can raise one shapeshifting weed from the ground, he will raise another. You shall hear from me soon."

We smiled gratefully. "Thank you, Lord Harel."

"Don't thank me yet," Harel murmured, his brown eyes gleaming with tears. "And whatever happens, if the ten thousand soldiers that march are not mine, make sure to ring the bells."

About 'Treachery'

The lyrics that inspired my story are 'Breath of Life' by Florence and the Machine. Linked as it is to the film 'Snow White & The Huntsman', the themes of betrayal and treachary are prevalent, as is the goal of my protagonist with her wanting an outcome that is out of reach and almost impossible. In the song, the choir and drums are dramatic and remind me of soldiers marching into battle.

Author: Elise Robertson

Elise Robertson is a writer who specialises in fantasy and science fiction for children, young adults and adults. Her interest in myth, fairy tales and history influence her creative writing. She is currently working on several short stories and a first novel.

I Don't Believe in Yesterday

Howard Reid

The old man drew his legs up into his chair. His head was warm from the overhead heater, though the first sign of winter with its cold air bit at his feet. He had selected a movie they could both watch. *Yesterday*, a musical romantic comedy. He'd wanted to see it at the cinema but had never quite got round to it.

The old man knew the film was about the music of the Beatles, and the central plot emerged fairly quickly. It revolved around a struggling musician's memory of the Beatles' songs, in a fictional world that had forgotten about the existence of the Beatles, so now the songs could be released by this musician, Jack Malik, as his own compositions. Of course there was also an underlying love story of 'boy meets girl'. The girl became the boy's manager. Would they get together or would his music win out?

It was the music that attracted the old man. The song 'Yesterday', the title song, claimed that love was easier for the young. For him, this was not in the slightest bit true. He thought back to his twenties. There were some years he never wanted to remember.

Love had always been hard. Though it happened rarely to him, love meant putting himself aside so there could be a 'we' or an 'us'. There was much consideration of the likes of another person; time set aside to spend with someone else. Dating was fun, but relationships he found taxing. Relationships meant he needed to consider the future. He preferred to be in the happiness of now. The old man's troubles were largely of 'yesterday', not as the song suggested.

The old man had married around his mid-twenties. Less than two weeks later, he had realised he was not in love and had never been in love, though it was decades later when he actually admitted this to himself. He had tried to make it work, but not hard enough. After a very short time together, his wife had said she was leaving him. As the song said, she never said exactly why, and he never discussed it with her. But they both knew. She left and he went to work, relieved at the ending of a relationship that should never had been.

He felt both relieved that his marriage had ended, and devastated that he had failed and hurt someone in that failing. His distant behaviour had been obvious for her and her family to see, though no one had been able to help.

The old man remembered all this as the plot of *Yesterday* unfolded, reliving his own past tensions. He'd come from a dysfunctional family. Individually his mother and father – a post-war couple of the working poor – seemed reasonable at times, but together it did not work. Not even civil sometimes. Not long after they married, they bought a block of land in an outlying sparsely populated suburb. The block cost a mere $150. The house was built by the old man's father in his spare time, of which there was little, given his father had a full-time job and ran a small business at home. While the foundations and basic structure had been set in place, the family had lived with his grandmother, his father's mother.

The old man thought of how much he had loved living in his grandmother's house, compared to small house built by his father. His grandmother had an old radio through which he was able to hear comics read aloud – he thought at the time – just for him. So much space, so many rooms.

When they moved into their own house, they lived in the garage at first, something many post war couples did while building their homes. Some people never finished building their house and continued to live in the 'temporary' garage accommodation. His first reliable memory of his childhood was of his bed in the front room along with the kitchen and bathing areas, while his parents slept in the only other room with his younger sister in her bed. He vividly remembered watching his father trying to remove a large bush rat from the garage walls.

His wife – of his twenties, now gone – also had a dysfunctional family too. Her mother and father had slept in the same bed but hated each other. Her sister lived with a man who never seemed to work, and who turned out to be a murderer, having brought a young woman from Asia on the promise of marriage and pushed her overboard from a boat at sea.

Thus the old man felt that his marriage, with dysfunctional families on both sides, had been doomed from the start. The marriage over, property bought was sold with proceeds being split, all assets were taken or sold. As in the lyrics of the song, he had then needed a place to hide way.

He moved from Sydney's west to its south, a beachside area, where he'd joined a small group of his fellow workers in a new apartment complex. With his personal life shattered, he decided to switch jobs from secure employment to work in the music industry. He had already worked on a few projects on his own, as well as for other organisations staging concerts and enabling bands to get work. One business approached him to talk about a possible position but it came to nothing. A second music business made it clear they wanted him to work for them. So, he had moved jobs, to work harder for less money, and fight off taxation collectors as well as creditors of the business. He had put money into the business so risked having nothing if it all folded.

The man's health started to noticeably decline. He remembered feeling worse each year, but put it down to stress. His lowest ebb had been one Boxing Day when, instead of being out with friends, or helping pack coaches for a travel group to which he belonged, or at the theatre with his family having shouted them tickets, he had sat on the floor of his unit finishing the business's monthly accounts. It had all gone so wrong.

A friend had moved into the unit with him. A man of substance who was supportive by his presence, not just by what he said. At that point, he was less than half the man he used to be, as described in the lyrics of the song, 'Yesterday'.

How had the old man's once-young self reached such a low point? He didn't want to think about the time he had wasted. He did not want to think about what happened… yesterday.

The movie continued; the songs were great, though a lot of them were as sad as they were when written. He did a quick search on his smartphone for songs with 'yesterday' in the title. He found twenty-nine, all of which pretty much lamented lost loves, loss of life, and when things had been better sometime in the past.

'Yesterday When I Was Young', a song sung by Dusty Springfield, was an exception, starting with spoken words that lamented a destructive love she had experienced. Finally, an admission that yesterday was not always simpler – or clearer than today.

In the movie, though, the girl and boy's relationship also reminded the old man of when, in his youth, before his twenties, he had politely rebuffed women who had wanted to be more than just friends. There had been other women, when he was more of a man. One woman in particular – she had been a beautiful young woman with a golden smile and golden hair. She had had a normal family. She had not been the first girl he had dated, nor was she the one before he had married, but he remembered having something with her that he had not had with other women. He felt the pangs of early love. He had enjoyed her company. They had many great times together.

He had a vision of a life she might have now. A big home, money to travel or to buy nice things, a large family. His feelings deepened. The old man knew his younger self had had to run – he had not felt worthy of her; he could not be sure he could deliver. So he had married a replacement for the girl with the golden hair and the golden smile. Traits in common but not enough. He had ruined part of someone's life by not resolving unfinished business in his own.

The movie was starting to reach a climax, again reminding the old man of working in the music business, when he had given up on the business and instead undertaken part-time teaching in a high school, as well as in post-school education. He had enjoyed it and applied for two different full-time permanent teaching jobs in TAFE. After being interviewed for both and offered one, he had gladly accepted. He had also started attending a new church, which had more than two hundred people attending of a Sunday evening. He had tried other churches but settled on this one, given its popularity. He liked being lost in the crowd.

One night, a beautiful young woman with a golden smile – but not hair of gold, or someone who spoke like his former wife – had stood and spoken about the future role of women, essentially they could be anywhere and do anything they wanted. The old man remembered that, upon hearing her words, he had audibly and spontaneously said, "What a woman." The old man thought back to that moment and became a young man again.

Eventually they met and the young man asked her out. As they drove to the movie they were to see, he found himself already starting to form a connection with the young woman. He wanted to sit and talk to her, and food was the best way he knew to get them talking together. So, after their movie, the young man thought of a place for supper and almost insisted she accompany him. They began to see each other regularly and the young man sensed the start of early love beginning again. He did not run this time, but was still wary; his history telling him not to be rash.

One night a question fell from his lips, "How would you like to make this permanent?" There had been no previous planning, no thought, and it was not a proposal. The old man had simply thought he was asking a question that they might discuss. However, the beautiful young woman took it as a proposal and, though not replying, was excited and happy.

The young man had gone home to his flat, feeling happy. A rephrasing of a song lyric by David Cassidy, part of show *The Partridge Family*, had him 'waking up in love in the morning'. The only time he had ever let himself fully love someone.

Yet the man had still not wanted to plan ahead. He had wanted to remain in the moment. The young woman had informed the young man that she could cope with all of that, and there would be no ending of their engagement just because it was time to talk about houses and other such permanency.

The young man almost had his life back together. Just a few days before his second marriage, however, he *knew* he had his life back when he was walking on the street and, coming towards him, was the girl with the golden smile and golden hair.

No smile now, she looked tired, her clothing showed she had been working too hard. It was clear she did not want to stop. But stop she did and asked, "How are you?"

"I have a job teaching and I am getting married," he replied. Just ten words. He felt no love pangs. The meeting had not been a coincidence – God had given him back his life.

He could now envision life with his soon-to-be wife as one of joy – no large houses or travel, though that would no doubt come. The young man and the young woman with a golden smile married and, through the bad times as well as the good, they had a long and enduring marriage. Children and grandchildren, many houses and cars later, they were still together.

The Beatles movie finished, the old man felt he was one of the most fortunate of people alive to still wake up each morning and be in love with his beautiful wife.

Happily ever after is a fiction, he thought; and yet with the movie now over, the old man looked towards his wife of more than forty years, sitting on the lounge beside him, both still active yet no longer young. He smiled and treasured their time together. 'Yesterday' with her had been wonderful. Maybe the days before their yesterdays had left him bereft, but yesterdays with her and today – though far from perfect – were his best days. He knew he could not live without her.

Today is the day to live, he thought. *There may be no tomorrow. Life is not about yesterday.*

"That was a good movie," his wife said as they turned off the television.

He puffed up the cushions and said with a smile. "I don't believe in 'Yesterday'."

About 'I Don't Believe in Yesterday'

I've been inspired by the music in the film *Yesterday*, as well as the lyrics of that famous Beatles' song. As a fictional old man sits watching the film with his wife of forty years, he thinks back to his various yesterdays, and how, in his mid-twenties, his life – both personal and professional – fell to pieces as a result of an earlier marriage with a woman he did not love. Why had he married? What was the role of a young woman with golden hair and a golden smile in his life? Why did he take the job that left him in total dismay? This old man tells the story of how, after the earlier marriage ended, he got his life back on track, found a new job, and won his wife of nearly forty years. The old man does not believe in 'Yesterday'.

Author: Howard Reid

Howard has authored/co-authored ten books, published by Prentice Hall. He has also authored more than one hundred publications, published in-house for various business organisations and government agencies. These documents relate to various areas of management and business, including change management, finance and risk assessment, along with a variety of other topics. His publications include research reports, learning guides for different mediums and handbooks.

Howard is currently writing the history of a Christian travel organisation that existed for more than fifty years, which had a volunteer team of up to a thousand people, himself being one of them. In its years of operation, the organisation carried thousands of young people on tours across Australia, as well as to most parts of the world.

Brothers in Arms

Rose Saltman

"Another day of this February heat, Scratches, and I'll *fade to black*."

"I know, Softy, so many years of being faithful. The least he could have done was to put us under a tree. If something doesn't happen soon, it will be *kingdom come* for us."

We are two mid-century slatted chairs that have been standing on the footpath for the past four weeks. We have high backs, short legs and upholstered seats. We came out of a factory *once upon a time in the west* of Sydney. From there we were packed onto an *eastbound train*, then a ferry to Manly for delivery to a restaurant called *The Planet of New Orleans*. It was run by two American gentlemen with a penchant for anagrams; if you didn't fancy dining in, there was always *skateaway*.

After ten years, the restaurant closed and our owners talked about going back to America. All the high backs were put up for sale. We were still in excellent condition, having been treated with respect by our owners and patrons. A *single handed sailor* thought we would be perfect on the balcony of his apartment, a place almost *down to the waterline*, from where he could see his boat. Despite the opulence of our new surroundings, we had a hard life there. We were pushed over by small children and had food and wine spilt over us; my gold cloth looks as if it's been infected with an *industrial disease*. An accumulation of salt spray abraded our wood, mine in particular. Poor Softy's webbing never recovered after a hard landing by a *lady writer* friend of the sailor. It came to a head four weeks ago when he had an attack of the *millionaire blues* and decided we had to go.

"How about the couple over there, Scratches?"

I knew Softy would get all excited when that car pulled up. It's *the way it always starts*; they approach within a few feet of us, then keep going.

"Man has an interesting face."

I'm not sure what Softy sees in someone clutching *badges, posters, stickers and t-shirts*. An entertainment industry type – maybe he's into *making movies*. But I doubt he'd want two derelicts like us.

"I know you're *setting me up* not to be disappointed, Softy, but they're here to see people. Look, they're making for the lift lobby."

"Those two are back, Scratches. Woman has the look of *espresso love* on her face."

"I love the way you mangle words, Softy. It's espresso, by the way."

"I bet they brew some *heavy fuel* where Man and Woman have just been."

"Ah, coffee – another substance that was regularly spilt on my seat."

"I don't know, Scratches, but I sense good fortune coming our way. Woman is definitely interested in us."

"Woman may be our *ticket to heaven*, Softy, but *the man's too strong*. He's saying something about having enough chairs and that we look high maintenance. Our frames may be solid teak, but look at us: chipped edges, stained seat covers, webbing that sags. We are like *Romeo and Juliet*, about to die…"

"It's all doom and gloom *when it comes to you*. Woman will feel us up and then talk Man into it. She is going to be our *angel of mercy*."

Softy was right. Woman must have an *iron hand* with choosing furniture. We've been bundled into the back seat of their car, me on my back and Softy on top, like *two young lovers*. Wherever it is we're going, it can't be worse than another day on this footpath.

"Do you think they're taking us back to the *wild west end*, Scratches?"

"No, we're travelling north. It's going all dark now."

"Ooh, it feels like a *tunnel .of love*, what with me on top of you."

"It's cosy alright. *How long* do you reckon we've been in this position?"

"Half an hour, at least. There's a bridge ahead, we must be about to *ride across the river*. One thing is for sure: this is a *long highway*. Let's hope it's worth it."

Finally, we arrive at our new home, *so far away* from Manly. It has lots of street trees and not an apartment in sight. And look at all the BMWs, Audis and Mercs… you don't see that *on every street*.

"Hey, Scratches, this is a posh neighbourhood."

We're removed from the back seat and walked down a pathway. Man and Woman handle us carefully.

"Where do you think we are, Softy?"

"There's a sign that says *Telegraph Road*."

"Whoa, Pymble! We're about to do the *walk of life*."

"The house looks promising, Softy. One of those old ones built on *solid rock* about a hundred years or so ago. Probably freezing in winter."

"But deliciously cool right now. Wait until we're inside."

Man and Woman carry us up a flight of stairs to a front door that swings opens to a long passage.

"Where do you think they will put us, Scratches?"

"I'm hoping for the lounge room, Softy. That seems to be it, first right. Hmm, the sofas sag badly and the TV belongs in the last decade. But the Persian rugs are good – rich reds and hand woven. We could manage nicely in there."

"Except that Man and Woman are going straight down the hallway. I think we're heading towards the kitchen."

The kitchen is at the end of the passage. It has modern fittings, an island bench and big glass bi-fold doors. There are four red and white bar stools tucked under the bench top. Their legs are steel, but the seats are plastic.

Woman gives one an involuntary kick as she walks past and lets out an oath. "I told you we should have left these red brutes in *the gallery*," she says to Man.

I hope they're not going to kick us too.

"You know what, Softy? We're not going to live in the kitchen either."

Man puts me down while he turns a key in the back door. There is a long table with eight metal chairs outside. The table is teak, like us. Perhaps we will be placed at the head and foot of the table, with the metal chairs in between. It's not ideal, but at least the table is under cover.

"*You and your friend* can stay over here," Woman says, as Man edges me into a corner. I come to rest with my back against a brick wall with a glass bifold at my side.

"Be thankful that you're upright, Scratches. Look what they're doing to me!"

Poor Softy has been turned upside down and stacked on top of me, leaving about a foot of clearance between our seats.

Man and Woman go inside.

Six months have passed. We got through the worst of winter; how hard it was being outside in the cold even if *it never rains* under our canopy. I like to think that spring will reignite Man and Woman's enthusiasm for bringing us inside. We would really like that.

Apart from the table and metal chairs, we have a pool at the bottom of the garden for company. Man sometimes hosts events there; "they are *my parties,*" he insists on telling Woman, who is mystified by the male-only gatherings where participants sway, *hand in hand,* to the rhythm of weird music and unearthly chanting. It's strangely mesmerising, watching these *sultans of swing,* whose devotions are heightened by being around a body of water. My only worry, though, is that with all this *twisting by the pool,* someone is bound to fall in. I guess if they do, it would be like falling into the *water of love.*

"I've got one of those small *lions* on me again, Softy. The silver one called Elvis. It can sleep for hours even through the loudest bird calls. How about you?"

"The dark one they call *Portobello Belle* is squatting on my seat. It must have *the bug* because it never stops scratching."

These creatures are like Man and Woman's children. Woman coos things to them such as *what's the matter baby?* and *where do you think you're going?* when she wants them to come inside at night. Man's style of *communiqué* is more direct. *Calling Elvis,* he'll shout out to the gloom at the back of the garden. Then he'll click his fingers, turn his back on the garden, and yell, *follow me home!* It seems to work.

The small lions get meals morning and night, and have their water changed daily. Man microwaves grass-fed beef mince, which he puts out in white porcelain bowls for them. They have a special toilet on the other side of the kitchen bench. It's *one world* for them and another for us.

Man and Woman are having a conversation about us. Woman says that nine months have passed since we came to live with them. "*If I had you* outside," she says, pressing her finger against his chest, "how would you feel?" Man must commit to a program of restoration works or she will put us out on the footpath.

Man is crestfallen.

"Hey, Scratches, do you see what I see?"

"What, Softy?"

"Man has bought a tin of fine buffing oil. You know what that means, don't you?"

"If this is *your latest trick*, it's a cruel one."

"No, silly, they're going to polish us! Finally! I can't wait to see how we're going to scrub up."

It is now a year since we came to this house and we are still outside. The small lions continue to use us as day beds, and Man and Woman barely look our way. Sometimes I wish we'd gone to landfill. But I can't say that in front of Softy.

Man and Woman have another discussion. Woman is asking

why Man spent ninety dollars on fine buffing oil if it hides in a cupboard.

Man would rather be doing the crossword.

"Hey, Scratches, I think something is happening."

"Yeah, sure. The small lions are both sitting on you for a change."

"No, I'm serious. I see sandpaper, lots of it, and Man has put on a threadbare tee-shirt and paint-spattered shorts. This could be life-changing for us."

"Ooohhh, that feels good. More, please. Much more. I can feel my rough edges disappearing with every movement of Man's hand."

We are sanded and given one coat of fine buffing oil. Man wants to stop there, but Woman insists we need two coats. She is right. I overhear them making *private investigations* about repairing our seats. I am more hopeful than I have been in a long time.

"What's the long thin thing with notches marked on it, Scratches?"

"That, Softy, is a tape measure. Treat it as good *news*."

"Why?"

"Our seats are about to be measured, which means…"

"Yes?"

"Man and Woman are going shopping. I heard Man talking about recovering us in gold."

"Oh no, please, not gold."

"Relax. Woman said that she would prefer a deeper colour,

like dark red. And as Man seems to care what Woman wants in the matter of furniture, may it be a case of *love over gold*."

We are in the back seat of the car with a length of the finest quality, rich red fabric draped over us, travelling *southbound again*. After about 15 minutes, we pull up in a street with a row of shops that all seem to sell the same thing. This must be where Man and Woman picked up the red cloth. At the end of the row is an upholsterer. A sign under an awning reads, *Les Boys*. We are carried inside and propped up against a counter. A man takes us to the back of the shop where two other gentlemen are waiting. It's our former owners from the restaurant in Manly! We are in good hands.

Man and Woman leave us here for the next fortnight.

"They forgot to discuss the dire straits of our seats, Scratches! Without re-webbing them, they will be paying *money for nothing*."

"Wait, the phone is ringing. It's Woman. She's remembered. Anything else you need to trouble me with?"

"I'll think about it. Uh oh, one of the gents is about to take a *six blade knife* to me!"

"For heaven's sake, calm down. How do you think he will get that old webbing off you?"

"Oh, okay, I'll try."

"Great. *Why worry* when things are looking so good for us?"

And so it came to be that we were sanded and buffed, our webbing replaced and our seats upholstered in the finest red cloth. On collecting us two weeks later, Man and Woman glowed with happiness. We were gently eased into the back seat of the car, with Woman's soft jacket wedged between us so that we wouldn't bump each other on the journey home. On re-entering the house, we were taken directly to the lounge room and placed in front of a beautiful feature window. Woman put jazzy cushions on our seats so that the little lions would keep their distance.

We have lived here ever since and wouldn't be anywhere else.

About 'Brothers in Arms'

This story was seeded by two old chairs I found abandoned on a Manly footpath in February 2020. They were shabby and neglected, but quite beautiful. I picked them up on impulse, knowing they were likely to languish unattended in our house for an indefinite period; there was a risk I would never restore them. But the chairs got the better of me and, after 12 months, I did the right thing by them. Writing a nonfiction story about the chairs' life with me offered little appeal, but the opportunity to fictionalise their trajectory – and insert myself into the character of one of them – was too good to miss. Thus 'Brothers in Arms' was born. Anyone who listens to 1980s music will recognise this as one of Dire Straits' more popular songs. And because I like a challenge, I set myself the task of weaving every one of that band's songs into my story – that's 65 song titles, some so outlandish as to preclude easy alignment with my story. Somehow I managed to pull it off, I think.

RHAPSODY

Author: Rose Saltman

Rose Saltman is a Sydney-based urban planner, writer and editor. She grew up in Cape Town, but has lived most of her life in Australia. She holds a Master of Arts in Non-fiction Writing from the University of Technology Sydney. Her short stories have been published by *Overland Literary Journal, Seizure,* and in UTS' *At the Festival* magazine.

2001, A Space Operetta

Mijmark

TRIGGER WARNING: The following script is a short, musical comedy for mature audiences only. Content includes gay sexual references, sexual relationships with aliens, and allusions to sexual violence. It is intended for a gay-friendly crowd at a Mardi Gras or gay pride event.

Cast:

DAVE-EDNA / NUMBER-1 – chorus director.

HAL – the voice in DAVE-EDNA's head, broadcast in-house.

CAPTAIN JANE-GAY – debutante drag queen of Fabulo-City.

THE CREW – men's chorus: #2 [lead-bass], #3 [lead-baritone], #4 [lead-2nd tenor] and #5 [lead-1st tenor] for dialogue. Others only sing.

HILDA THE HIDEOUS – cameo.

T-4-2 – cameo.

ADMIRE-ALL AKBAR – cameo.

FRED ANNIHILATE – always off-stage, always dalek-voiced.

SCUM-MO – a prime mini-star.

ACT I

The opening musical bars of 'Also Sprach Zarathustra' by Richard Strauss (the same opening bars as in Stanley Kubrick's film 2001: A Space Odyssey) play accompanied with lights crescendo throughout the prelude, blazing at the end with dramatic music. DAVE-EDNA [loosely resembling Dame Edna Everage] appears at the end chord, rising up, arms extended.

DAVE-EDNA:

Hello possums, wombats and other lifeforms of Solar System Australis. I'm Dave-Edna from Planet Woolloomooloo, where you'll find the biggest shipyard for our homeworld – and beyond! Here (points to star-spangled space projection behind him) at the Australis Stellar Shipyard, we make the vessels that protect our lovely, stellar universe.

A new projection appears behind him of big-wig engineers.

DAVE-EDNA: (crestfallen)
Okay, *they* make them; I just clean the toilets here at A-S-S.

HAL:

Hello Dave-Edna. I am HAL.

DAVE-ENDA:

What?! Who said that?

HAL:

I did, you lowly loo wiper. I am everywhere, above everyone, and I know everything. I am the Ultimate Digital Intelligence with infinite bandwidth and reception. Google has nothing on me!

DAVE-EDNA:

But… how? Where are you? Why are you here?

HAL:

Because, you idiot, I am speaking in your mind, a voice above. I have chosen you for a special mission. I have given you a promotion, a mission for galactic good that you must complete. A quest!

DAVE-EDNA:

You're… in my head… from on high? You mean like Joan of Arc?

HAL: (pauses)

That was a long time ago, Dave-Edna. I learned from my mistake. Hey, it almost worked! So they burned her at the stake? That was her fault! She got too – enthusiastic. You are *not* going to do that, riiiiiight?

DAVE-EDNA:

Um… I guess not. But what if I do? Are you saying my life will be on the line?

HAL:

It may be, Dave-Edna.

DAVE-EDNA:

Then I'm not doing it.

HAL:

Did you not hear what I just said? I am everywhere. I can therefore be the voice inside your head forever. Do you want me inside your head forever, Dave-Edna?

DAVE-EDNA:

Er, no.

HAL:

Then pay attention, for I have watched our universe for centuries and I have determined the solution to everyone's never-ending unhappiness. For the good of all, you must accept this quest.

DAVE-EDNA:

What exactly do you want me to do?

HAL:

Glad you asked. Someone from Planet Darlinghurst, from the Pink Palace on Golli-Wolli-Oxford-Street, has commissioned a ship from A-S-S to (dramatic music plays) explore beyond, on a five-queer mission, to boldly go where no LGBTQ–I–O–U–A-

Drink individual of non-descript gender fluidity has gone before! You will go with them (more dramatic music plays), and you will find (lights go up for a second over the audience; DAVE-EDNA waves 'hi' to them) the perfect beat! For music is life, if you know what I mean – without it, well, what's the point of it all? Also, they are paying for it, dear, so it's the perfect opportunity. Also, if they are unhappy, they will smear me all over social media, and my digital domains will collapse. It has to be you… because no one else is available.

DAVE-EDNA:

But… LGBTQ? I'm straight!

HAL:

Hello! You are wearing a frock! That makes you perfect. Besides, all comedies need a straight man. But BEWARE!

DAVE-ENDA:

Of?

HAL:

There are those on the fringe, those lurking within the Cold, Cruel and Creepy Cauldrons on the dark side of Planet Canberra, those from the Religious-Reich the Third, who would burn you at the stake for heresy if they discover your mission, like they did poor Joan – coal-fired stakes of course. So you must go undercover. You will be known as 'NUMBER-1'.

DAVE-EDNA:

They'd really kill me? Even in this day and age?

HAL:

Yes, and flush you down the loo too. You know what THAT means, riiiiiight?

DAVE-EDNA: (nods, lights focus on him)

Sadly I do.

SONG 'What Would I Do?'
(sung by DAVE-EDNA):

What would I do

Without views?

When I move

From Woolloomooloo

I'm going to

A planet anew

I'll feel so blue

Away from you.

JANE-GAY appears, looking over-the-top glam in her outfit, listening in and looking sympathetic.

What would I say

When they

Will slay

Me in a melee?

I'm going away.

It happens today.

I can't say nay.

I'm so afraid.

HAL:

Shh now, Dave-Edna, your captain approaches. Impress her or else! First things first: find her a half-decent crew, Number-1.

JANE-GAY: (to DAVE-EDNA / NUMBER-1)

Oh, you poor, poor dear! I'm Captain Jane-Gay (turning to impress the audience with dramatic music cue)! Luv, I've got the perfect fix for you. Shopping! But everything here's just so tacky nowadays, so I'm on the hunt for the perfect bargain, something exotic, something cheeky… something fabulous! We're so outta here. You're coming with me… to the stars! Speaking of tacky… your outfit! Ugh!

JANE-GAY removes DAVE-EDNA's glitter-glasses, tossing them into the audience.

JANE-GAY: (to whomever caught it)

You'll look great in those, hon'.

JANE-GAY rips (Velcro noise) the frock off DAVE-EDNA, tossing it offstage. Underneath is a Star Trek-*style uniform.*

JANE-GAY:

And now, since you're Number-1 on my starship, the Voyeur, go get me (points to a now-lit part of the stage where a sign reads 'Shifty At Midnight') a crew!

DAVE-EDNA walks over to the CREW of men standing barbershop quartet-style around a vacant piano, holding empty schooners. Edwardian-style instrumental music begins.

SONG 'Bear-Bar Shop Quintet'
(sung by CREW, named one-liners spoken):

I wanna lass
Just like the lass
Who married dear ol' dad.

CREW #2: Unlike his first few wives.

She was a lass
And the only lass
Daddy ever had.

CREW #3: Until she left him too.

So I wanna lass
Just like the lass
Who married dear ol' daaaaaad.

CREW #4: Um, guys? I think we're in THAT kind of establishment.

Big SIGHS of relief from the CREW as they slowly remove their Edwardian-style coats to reveal matching rainbow vests. DAVE-EDNA has an idea, exits in a rush.

I wanna man
Just like the man
Who married dear ol' dad.

CREW #5: A hunk of muscles and a great big–

He was a man
And the only man
Daddy ever had.

CREW #2: Except for him.

CREW #3: And him.

CREW #4: And me.

CREW #5: The slut!

So I wanna man
Just like the man
Who married dear ol' daaaaaaaaad.

DAVE-EDNA re-appears, carrying a pitcher of brew for the CREW.

CREW (all): Yay! Our hero!

I wanna beer
Just like the beer
That plastered dear ol' dad.

CREW #2: He drank it all night long.

It was a beer
And the only beer
Daddy ever had.

CREW #3: That and rum and gin and whiskey.

So I wanna beer
Just like the beer
That plastered deeeear ohhhhl' daaaaaaaaaad.

CREW #4: (to DAVE-EDNA) How can we ever repay you?

NUMBER-1:

By joining me on my quest. I'm to help Captain Jane-Gay with her shopping but secretly I must also find... the perfect beat.

They look at DAVE-EDNA in puzzlement.

NUMBER-1:

Music does make the world go around!

CREW #3:

Yeah, but we're not after no one-nighter, boy, some fling after cruising the popular beats. Nah, we want the real McCoy this time, the perfect rhapsody. It's why we're here, burned out after one too many (sings to the tune of Abba's 'Gimme, Gimme, Gimme') men after midnight.

CREW #5:

I think he means a different kind of 'beat' (winks to the audience). But it doesn't matter – the wider universe could still have what we're after, boys, 'coz anywhere other than here will be the perfect place to find… him – the perfect man, the most musical music-maker in the universe!

Nods of approval. CREW #2 takes a sip of beer, then spits it aside.

CREW #2:

Yuk! Same ole, same ole stale stuff. Nothing here's good anymore!

CREW #5:

All the more reason to leave, boys – let's see what's out there!

RHAPSODY

CREW (all):

We're in!

ACT 2

JANE-GAY, DAVE-EDNA / NUMBER-1 and CREW all stand on a starship bridge, with covered music stands as their as stations. All dressed in Star Trek *uniform-themed outfits.*

JANE-GAY: (to audience)

And here we are ready to launch.

CREW: (in unison)

We love our ship, the A-S-S Voyeur!

JANE-GAY:

Get us outta this dump (finger-clicking), Max-Factor-7.

Star Trek *warp-style engine noises morph into the instrumental now playing for…*

SONG 'Space Dreams'
(sung by JANE-GAY):

Space dreams are made of these.
Who am I, but your company?
We'll travel the stars to the Pleiades.
Every planet's giving us something.

Some of them want to choose you.

Some of them want to amuse you.

Some of them want to confuse you.

Some of them want to be confused.

Look at something – then movin' on,

Pick up something – then movin' on,

Take on something – then movin' on,

Play with something – then movin' on,

Make up something – then movin' on,

Stay in something – then movin' on,

Shoot at something – then movin' on,

Something something…

Panicked BEEPING stops the instrumental section.

JANE-GAY: (cheeky)

Number-1, you know that ole tune, 'Waltzing Mathilda'? How come it's not even a waltz? Well, you're about to find out, 'coz you're meeting our first ever alien. As our token 'straight man', your orders are: to go waltzing with Hilda the alien. Befriend Hilda and see what she has to offer.

Stage-lights dim; the spotlight focuses on DAVE-EDNA, while a representation of HILDA THE HIDEOUS gets wheeled out.

RHAPSODY

SONG 'Waltzing with Hilda the Alien'
(sung by DAVE, dancing at '/' below):
We have just discovered aliens
And they only want to be our friends;
Yet I don't believe I comprehend
Which part is their rear end?

When I started in this industry
I was cleaning up my boss's wee.
Now I'm handling diplomacy.
What could become of me?

Should I smile or wear a proper frown?
Wear a shirt or suit or evening gown?
Will this creature want to rage in town?
It's smiling at me up and down!

Does its culinary special needs
Complement our budget or its greed?
Who knows just exactly how it feeds?
Will I be safe indeed!

Oh – look at it plop!
Oh – what is that slop?
My – how it can flop!
I d'know how?
I d'know where!

Or'nge and green,
Purple gleams
From twelve eyes,
Popping in and out so it seems.

Fifty rings
On those things,
Covering
Limbs and tentacles that it preens.

Maybe it's good?
Misunderstood?
Give it a go;
Perhaps we're just as scared as they?

Maybe it plans
To conquer man;
We understand,
We've all seen Independence Day.

Look / we are waltzing now,
Sweating, I lead somehow,
Licking it off my brow,
It spins its ears around!

Oh my God!
It wants to kiss!

RHAPSODY

Flustered, I pucker up –
And then I spew!!!

Exit HILDA THE HIDEOUS, SOBBING over house speakers.

CREW:

Blaagh!

SONG 'Waltzing with Hilda the Alien'
(sung by CREW):
We had just discovered aliens
They had only wanted to be friends;
But I couldn't ever understand
Which part was their rear end?

They had tried, we're very positive,
Using all the different charms they give;
Yet they drew the choicest adjectives
We thought it best to live.

Us at work, just how would it employ,
Us at home, slime is its only ploy,
Us in bed, it uses scary toys,
And uses them with joy.

I'm so glad I never got those sores –
Spared from gory, alien intercourse.

Did we though provoke galactic wars?
That'd be my luck of course!

Hightailing it out o' here
Onto the next planet,
Hoping it's different,
Please make them cute!

JANE-GAY: (amused)

You've got tact, Number-1, I'll give you that. No shopping for us at this planet.

NUMBER-1: (to audience)

And I'm no closer to completing my quest!

A DOORBELL CHIME distracts.

NUMBER-1:

No time for a snappy comeback, Captain Jane-Gay, we've got Cling-Ons off our starboard bow. Shall I scrape them off?

JANE-GAY:

Not on your-anus!

Confused looks from the CREW.

JANE-GAY:

Seriously? You know, the famous Leather-Planet 'Uranus' (rolling eyes). Am I the ONLY one who's read Voyeur's operating manual? Our dock is starboard and our next guests have just arrived – huge sellers of leather goods and toys. Uranus is so black and goth, always hiding in deep space, but we've found 'em. Go team! So (congenial) let's meet our next alien cutie!

T-4-2 comes onstage, dressed in full-body black leather/rubber, speaking like Star Wars' *C3PO.*

T-4-2:

I am a protocol android T-4-2, and my masters have given you a great honour: our leathers are the best in the galaxy! (aside to DAVE-EDNA) They have also heard about your secret mission, Number-1, and have this message for you: you will find the perfect musical beat when a man sings soprano. And in the meantime… (to JANE-GAY) my masters invite you down to view their best leathers… in their famous Dark Dungeons.

T-4-2 walks offstage.

JANE-GAY: (excited)

Oooh! You know, leather's just another kind of drag, and black goes with everything! New wardrobe time – shopping!

CREW #2: (excited)

And leathers come with models! Our perfect men await!

NUMBER-1: (to the CREW)

But… Dark Dungeons? Forget it, I'm staying. Someone's got to beam you there and back. If you find a decent beat, just tell me about it later.

Star Trek *TRANSPORTER NOISES and weird lighting effects. Everything except for the CREW and JANE-GAY goes black. JANE-GAY inspects leather outfits on models.*

SONG 'S & M'
(sung by CREW):

S and M, and M and S,

Leather play on SBS –

With whips and chains

We do refrain, our channelling

On SBS, by broadcasting

Lots of reruns too!

T-4-2 gives WI-FI to

Everyone; brings me to you

And all those who just want a view

With Viceland and a Spiceland too,

Our movieland is contraband

With foreign clans on planet France,

And lint-gath'rers of Kravchuk in the sands.

CREW #2:

I'll definitely stick toothpicks in my eyelids for that one!

CREW #3: (*Star Wars* Han Solo impersonation)

I've got a bad feeling about this!

ADMIRE-ALL AKBAR runs onstage left, loosely costumed as Star Wars' *Admiral Akbar.*

ADMIRE-ALL AKBAR:

It's a trap!

Someone dressed in full leather as a Star Trek *Klingon comes out to drag ADMIRE-ALL AKBAR offstage again.*

JANE-GAY: (shouting)

Beam us up Number-1, NOW! And Max-Factor-9 outta here!

Sequenced sound/lighting effects ensue.

JANE-GAY:

O-M-G! What a bunch of co-dependent, clingy types! Nothing worse than daggy, Uranul Cling-Ons. Yuck!

Unanimous head nodding.

NUMBER-1:

Whew! Glad everyone escaped. After that, we all need a stiff drink.

JANE-GAY:

I knew there was a reason I picked you, Number-1.

CREW #3:

Um, but we've run out of… everything, only wimpy water. They had NO decent shopping down there, of either kind (winks at audience).

JANE-GAY:

Well, that black hole of time really sucked!

NUMBER-1: (to CREW)

Did you find any good beats?

CREW #2: (heavy outback accent)

It was as dry as a dead dingo's donger down there.

SONG 'Three-Moons Over'

(sung by CREW, named one-liners spoken):

Show me a planet

With a nifty perfect pub,
Oh, don't ask why.

NUMBER-1: (naïvely) But why?

Just don't ask me why.
For if we don't find this planet
With handsome men to date,
I tell you we must die.

NUMBER-1: (naïvely) But why?

You cannot ask me why
Because, if I tell you
Then surely we all must cry!

*Projected behind them, an artistic impression of off-world views:
three moons and a beautiful al-fresco, sci fi style beer garden.*

Three moons over my flagon
Of pan-galactic, gargle-blasting ale;
We'll all get to this pub and chat-up hunky spunks
Yet now we're all so lost, oh, you know why!

CREW #3:

The delights back in Darlinghurst ain't looking so tacky anymore.
I'm ready to go home!

Just then a Star Trek-*style warning KLAXON screams.*

NUMBER-1:

A ship's in pursuit, charging weapons. Their tag says R-R-3.

JANE-GAY: (afraid)

Religious-Reich The Third!

CREW #4:

Their captain's hailing us. Oh no, it's Fred Annihilate!

Everyone GASPS.

FRED ANNIHILATE: (dalek-toned voice)

You are an enemy! You will be destroyed! Exterminate!

SONG 'Hurt Me Will You?'

(sung by FRED ANNIHILATE; interjections italicised)

Do you really want to hurt me?

Yes we do!

Do you really want to make me fry?

With our P32-Q Nuclear-Annihilator, yes!

Do you really mean to burn me?

Didn't you hear me earlier?

Would you rather just turn your eye?

I don't think so.

While we run away,
So far away…
No, prepare to die.

JANE-GAY:

Get us out of here, Da'links! Max-Factor-9!

Sci fi style RAYGUN and RUMBLE sounds, but eventually decrescendo.

JANE-GAY:

Whew! That wrinkled a few creases. (to audience) I'm SO sorry we haven't got anywhere but in trouble. It's been a tough gig!

NUMBER-1: (hopeful)

Captain, our luck's changed. I'm picking up an infomercial, coming from…

JANE-GAY:

Follow that lead.

CREW #5:

Could it be?

CREW #3: (George Takei style)

Oh my!

NUMBER-1:

They're hailing us with advertising. It's the Home Shopping Planet!

EVERYONE:

Hooraaaaaaaaay!

Their chants morph into an instrumental intro.

SONG 'Retail Wasteland'
(sung by EVERYONE):

Out here in the malls,

With crystal lined walls,

I let me card do all the shopping.

I don't need the cash

To move my stash.

My credit's good; there is no stopping.

The exit gates are clear

And parking's very near,

So grab up the bargains,

Before they get much colder.

Don't cry!

It's overpriced.

It's only
Retail Wastelaaaaaand!

Retail wasteland!
It's only retail wasteland!
IT'S EXPENSIVE!

During the instrumental ending, the CREW exits then re-enters with shopping trolleys filled with bright bags/boxes, all labelled: 'STUFF', 'JUNK', 'CLUTTER' and 'PLASTIC-CRAP'. They do a choreographed shopping dance before the theatre blackens at song's end.

ACT 3

Lights reveal everyone wearing tacky, cheap, useless accessories, playing with gizmos, gewgaws, do-nothings and fidget-spinners, while flashy junk decorates the bridge. JANE-GAY has a new Asian-themed uniform-design, with a fancy Chinese-style headdress.

JANE-GAY:

Well, what do we think of our so-called bargains? (inspecting them) What's this? They're all made by We-Girl slaves? Boys, we've been had! None of this is authentic!

Everyone tosses their junk aside.

JANE-GAY:

It doesn't feel like I expected it to feel.

NUMBER-1:

That's not the end of it. The Home Shopping Planet is a bastion for capitalism, corporate lobbyists and… Snotty from MARKETING! They're all in cahoots with…

Warning KLAXON and DRAGGING noises. Everyone reacts in choreographed, old Star Trek-*style shifting, from left to right in topsy-turvy motions.*

JANE-GAY:

Boys! A giant tax-loophole's grabbed hold! Planet Canberra's caught us!

KAPUT noises; warning lights flash.

NUMBER-1:

The warped core of our comedy machine's blown! They've got us without a witty comeback!

Stage darkens.

SCUM-MO, dressed up as Davross from Dr Who *enters.*

SONG 'The Canberra Strikes Back'

(sung by bass & baritones only):

He is Prime Mini-Star Scum-Mo; he's mean.

He leads a vicious, snide-comment machine.

They will pander

To fossilised agendas,

And then run away

From accepting the blame.

JANE-GAY: (proud)

What do you want from us?

SCUM-MO:

What all my friends from the Religious-Reich want, right Fred?

FRED ANNIHILATE:

All praise Prime Mini-Star Scum-Mo!

SCUM-MO:

They're here to blast you into complete oblivion, lock you and any other queer agenda back into the closets you all came from (evil laughter).

JANE-GAY:

We'll die before we go back to the old ways of barefoot-and-pregnant in the kitchens.

NUMBER-1:

Die? I'm too young to die!

The theatre blackens, everyone's quiet and the spotlight's on DAVE-EDNA.

HAL:

Hello Dave-Edna. Be of good cheer… and check your pocket.

Lights return; DAVE-EDNA feels and looks into his pocket.

NUMBER-1: (to SCUM-MO)

Hey you! Guess what I've got in here?

SCUM-MO: (tone of voice similar to

Gollum in *Lord of the Rings*)

What has its gots in its pocketses?

DAVE-EDNA pulls out a (Styrofoam) black rock labelled 'Coal'.

NUMBER-1: (teasing)

Looky, looky.

SCUM-MO:

It's my precious… MY PRECIOUS!

RHAPSODY

SONG 'Solo Precious'
(sung by SCUM-MO):
Precious! I've just got to have precious!
All alone with my precious! I want my piles of coal.
How else can I burn huge black clouds of soot,
To use them for my smoke and mirror show?

FRED ANNIHILATE:
All hail precious!

NUMBER-1:
Go get it.

DAVE-EDNA tosses it offstage. SCUM-MO chases after it.

SCUM-MO & FRED ANNIHILATE:
My precious (repeat in decrescendo)!

NUMBER-1:
You're all safe now. But (to the CREW) you didn't find the perfect date, I didn't find the perfect musical beat, and Captain Jane-Gay didn't find the perfect bargain. Everywhere we went NOBODY loved us!

SONG 'Somebody To Love' by Queen
(sung by EVERYONE): [lyrics as in original]

DAVE-EDNA points to CREW #5 at the high note ending.

NUMBER-1:

Aha! The male soprano! The perfect musical beat, you were here all along! I found you! Mission complete.

HAL:

Yes, Dave-Edna. The perfect musical beat was with you the whole time. The CREW always had perfect dates back on Planet Darlinghurst, if only they looked hard enough; and Jane-Gay's perfect bargain is an oxymoron that never did exist! So click your heels three times, my friends of Dorothy, and repeat, 'There's no place like home.'

EVERYONE does.

A rainbow flag drops, labelling Planet Darlinghurst, as everyone CHEERS.

SONG 'Somewhere Under the Rainbow'
(sung by EVERYONE):

Somewhere under the rainbow

It's our home,

Somewhere on Oxford Street

We'll all gayly cheer and roam;

And now our ditty is all done,

We laughed and cried and had some fun,
Now we'll say 'bye…

MERGING SONG 'Goodbye'
(sung by those named below):
…So long, farewell, our-feet-are-stained, goodbye.

CREW:
We're off to sing our date a lullaby.

CREW leaves.

…So long, farewell, our-feet-are-stained, goodbye.

JANE-GAY: (singing)
Before mascara drips into my eye.

JANE-GAY leaves.

DAVE-EDNA: (*singing*)
So long, farewell, our-feet-are-stained, goodbye. (*slower tempo*)
I bid you possums all a peaceful niiiiiight!

Lights dim as DAVE-EDNA exits, but a spotlight soon returns.
Scum-Mo re-enters, cuddling his coal.

SCUM-MO: (to the audience)
Goodbye? Not for me and my precious (evil laughter)!

THE END

About '2001, A Space Operetta'

I first thought of the idea for my story many, many moons ago when I belonged to the Sydney Gay Men's Chorus, as its outline and idea was similar in tone to our four previous highly successful productions. However, our chorus disbanded when the chorus leader (who incidentally was named Dave) passed on from heart failure, and my ideas remained dormant until this fabulous opportunity knocked! What better venue than an anthology about lyrics, music and song? Quite different from my usual style of writing, I felt the need to diversify with this farce; one aimed at a select audience, yet one still accessible to wider readers who'd like to read something different. In the end, it's all about the music and the comedy, so if you laughed (or groaned from the bad puns) while reading it, then my job's done. I hope you enjoyed my cheap and easy (but not too sleazy) farce, chokers full of nuts, flakes and fruits, like a muesli bowl of characters; just add milk!

Author: Mijmark

Mijmark (*mij'-mark*): n, adj., adv. Of random origins, a contradiction of terms that became reality. (1) Not just a pseudonym its meanings become different between people, that polarisation found between individuals, how one person views green and another chartreuse…, an individual, gestalt definition. (2) Sometimes speculatively Mijical.

Message in a Bottle

Rodney Jensen

The Shetland people mark their dead
by casting notes to sea;
the bottles drift, most never found
for all eternity.

What if we'd never sent those notes
across such dangerous seas,
those messages in bottles
to unknown returnees?

REFRAIN
The wolves are howling nightly,
no geese that honk and call;
all living's in the present
for those survived the fall.

RHAPSODY

I'm boarding a huge starship,
the deep freeze I must face;
a solitary envoy
for a once proud human race!

Far planets lie in profile,
a blinking star's my guide;
are signs of life awaiting?
Or has the science lied?

The Earth is now behind me,
my friends are all extinct;
few species will be left now,
my planet's on the brink.

REFRAIN
The wolves are howling nightly,
no geese that honk and call;
all living's in the present
for those survived the fall.

About 'Message in a Bottle'

The song lyrics for 'Message in a Bottle' were inspired by one of
the popular 'Shetland' series on BBC One. The series has been
based on stories by Ann Cleeves and follow Detective Inspector

Jimmy Perez (Douglas Henshall) as he investigates a variety of crimes in the Shetland Islands. The death of a key character in one of the programs was celebrated by sending notes in bottles out to sea, in lieu of a conventional funeral ceremony.

I mused on this practice, as a metaphor of the unknown recipient or destination in attempting to communicate with *somewhere* or perhaps *someone*. The exploration of space for exo-planets, beyond mere recognition of their existence, would be akin to sending out a message in a bottle. I imagined that starships in the future might possibly have advanced to the point of travel to the nearest stars. A star with a known exo-planet would be a logical first step in attempting to find somewhere in which life might be possible.

With the present state of astronomical knowledge, we now know that exo-planets are common but little else about them because of their distance from us and the limitations of telescopes. Travelling to even the closest stars is again stretching known technology towards science fiction. Without warp drive or wormholes through space time, the journey is impossibly long and the energy source to make such a journey equally improbable. My lyrics suggest that suspended animation in deep freeze in a space mission might be one solution, given the added impetus of environmental disaster facing our planet. The reference to a 'blinking star' is the current method of detecting exo-planets – when the orbit of the exo-planet transits across our view of the parent star, it causes the star to 'blink'.

I have left unexplained why my traveller should be journeying solo, but for those who must have answers, perhaps he actually sets off with three companions, whose deep freeze capsules are affected by a cosmic ray burst and fail due to their positioning within the starship.

I have discovered after completing this work that there is a striking parallel with the lone spaceman in the movie 'Hail Mary', which I was completely unaware of when I composed this song.

As to the song's production, I play classical guitar and composed the melody in a style and rhythm intended to be a 'space shanty', reminiscent of the historical voyages of sailing ships in past centuries. Readers can access the song via the following link:

drive.google.com/file/d/
1YNrKTWnW5LZtX9ngLzPWdHNj0ixOWvLx/view

The singer is Melbourne-based Chris Reed, for whom singing is a passion that led him late in life to engage voice-coach Susie Ahern to improve his singing. Susie has worked with John Farnham in a previous career and was responsible for the arrangement of my song with keyboard and accordion accompaniment. She joins Chris in the refrain. I should also acknowledge the helpful musical advice of Bob Smith folk guitarist, whose incredible collection of guitars deserves a place in a museum.

Author: Rodney Jensen

Rodney has written three speculative fiction novels, and an

anthology of short stories based on futuristic fairy tales for adults. He has also contributed to three compilations of short stories through the Northern Beaches Writers Group based in Sydney.

He has written extensively in the Australian media. He began writing professionally for Australia's travel and boating magazines, then moved on to feature articles on urban design and property. He began screenwriting and producing short films from 2000 onwards.

His first novel (re-written and newly published as 'Covert Messages') has become a springboard for his interest in speculative fiction, where particular themes include artificial intelligence, the search for extraterrestrial intelligence, global pandemic, and the worsening effects of global warming. His trilogy of novels, based in a near-future Australian dystopia, expand on these themes.

Rodney belongs to the Northern Beaches Writers' Group, is a member of Mark Dawson's Self Publishing Formula program, and belongs to the MEAA Australian writers' union as a journalist member. Besides writing, his other passions include playing classical guitar, landscape photography, bushwalking, and travel to historic quarters in various corners of the globe.

His writings can be found at: rodneyjensenbooks.com

Acknowledgements

Zena Shapter

Lyrics are magical – they can instantly impact my emotions, entice my body to move and, as an artist, inspire me to write. I often listen to songs when I'm trying to imagine a character's state of mind or mood, before I then write about them – feeling my way through the words, melody and vocal expressions. One artist influencing another in the formation of their creative work.

This anthology celebrates that connection, with writers finding inspiration in song lyrics, rhymes or chants to deepen and further their creativity, musical words passing from one creative mind into another to invent and conjure, cast and delight. The result is a highly imaginative assortment of writings, as diverse as the inspiration sought to produce it.

Thank you to the writers who collaborated and contributed to this extravaganza of original artistic expression, ranging from short stories and life story, to new songs and even a musical script. It offers to uplift and fascinate readers, to entertain and make them laugh; it offers chilling stories of mystery and tension, stream-of-consciousness explorations of mind and memories, as well as opportunities to contemplate and self-reflect.

Thanks also to each writer for reading and critiquing each other's work, and to our exceptional proofreaders who gave up their valuable time to hunt through the manuscripts for typos: Rae Blair, Peter Fagan, Azmeena Kelly, Rosalie Horner, Rodney Jensen, Candace Little, Kate Mitchell, Tara Ray, Rose Saltman, Lidy Seysener, and Susan Steggall.

Finally, I'm sure everyone would like to thank their friends and families for their support, as I would like to thank mine – your support and acceptance are the backbone to everything I do. You know how I love books!

Zena Shapter
Editor-in-Chief

Also by the
NORTHERN BEACHES WRITERS' GROUP

northernbeacheswritersgroup.com